"I'm pregnant. Th[ ]
months," Tommi s[ ]

There wasn't much that truly threw Max, anymore. Not about most people, and certainly not about himself. Yet, what caught him off guard just then was his gut-level reaction to what shouldn't have registered on that level at all.

The feel of her body had burned itself into his brain. Some shred of nobility, along with a hefty dose of self-preservation, hadn't allowed him to think too much about it, though. At least, not until now.

As his glance moved over her, he could too easily recall the feel of her curvy little shape. The fullness of her firm breasts had pressed his chest when he'd caught her against him. When his hand had slipped along her side as he'd lifted her and when he'd helped her sit down, he'd been intensely aware of the gentle, feminine curve of her hip.

Dear Reader,

The holidays.

For many of us, the phrase means sparkling lights, carols, scents of cedar and cinnamon. Preparations. Anticipation. Celebrations. Some years are hectic, festive but exhausting. Other years demand less of our time and resources but are equally, often even more, fulfilling.

Once in a while, though, it happens that the glitter and wonder of the joyous season barely registers, or gets lost completely when life becomes complicated.

That's what happened to Tommi Fairchild.

Tommi's wish for Christmas is simply to get through it—and to get her life in order before anyone discovers that she's preparing for a little bundle of joy of her own. But we all know that what we wish for doesn't always happen, or come about the way we plan.

This year, what she gets for Christmas is the fairy tale.

My wish is that life brings you wondrous surprises, too.

With love,

Christine

ONCE UPON A CHRISTMAS EVE

CHRISTINE FLYNN

SPECIAL EDITION

Published by Silhouette Books

America's Publisher of Contemporary Romance

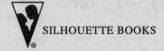

SILHOUETTE BOOKS

ISBN-13: 978-0-373-65568-7

ONCE UPON A CHRISTMAS EVE

Recycling programs
for this product may
not exist in your area.

Books by Christine Flynn

CHRISTINE FLYNN

admits to being interested in just about everything, which is why she considers herself fortunate to have turned her interest in writing into a career. She feels that a writer gets to explore it all and, to her, exploring relationships—especially the intense, bittersweet or even lighthearted relationships between men and women—is fascinating.

For every woman seeking her Prince Charming.

And for Allison, Lois and Pat.
Thanks again, ladies!

Chapter One

Tommi Fairchild had been raised to handle whatever she faced with grace, determination and calm.

She could manage grace as long as she suppressed her tendency to fidget or pace. Determination she'd always possessed, since she'd never have had the courage to go into business for herself without it. It was the calm part eluding her at the moment. As she watched the ebb and flow of guests moving past the ornately decorated Christmas tree in the Olympic Hotel's gorgeous, garland-draped lobby, she desperately tried not to feel…desperate.

Needing to distract herself from the anxiety causing her foot to jiggle, she consciously stilled the movement, straightened in the club chair she occupied and focused on the festive tree. Beyond it, a porter bundled against Seattle's damp first-of-December air pushed a luggage cart through the tall glass front doors.

The attempt at distraction lasted long enough for her to

wonder how much longer she could preserve the illusion that all was well in her once neatly ordered little world.

In the past two weeks, she'd been turned down by a credit union and two banks for a loan. Her prospects with a third bank weren't looking good, either—given that the loan officer hadn't returned her calls. Still, the optimist in her needed very much to believe that her luck with her dwindling prospects was about to change.

Yesterday, her Uncle Harry's secretary had called to tell her that a business associate of his had been quite impressed by the *Northwest Times'* latest review of her restaurant. That man wanted to see her as soon as possible.

Uncle Harry—her honorary uncle, actually, given that he was a family friend rather than related by blood—knew nothing of her predicament. No one did. Because she didn't want to worry her family, or suffer their inevitable disappointment in her before it became absolutely necessary, she needed to keep it that way. At least, until she could assure them that she had everything under control.

She barely knew the man who'd asked for this meeting. Harry had introduced her to Scott Layman last month at a Hunt Foundation dinner, a not-so-intimate affair for three hundred of Seattle's key corporate and social movers and shakers. Scott had been among the glitterati. He was the Layman of Layman & Callahan, the international consulting firm Harry's people used to locate properties worldwide for the expansion of his multi-billion-dollar computer company.

Of more importance to her at the moment, as she'd learned from their website last night, Layman & Callahan also invested in local businesses as part of its commitment to the community.

Since it had been the glowing review that had caught his interest, she could only believe that, at the very least, Scott was looking for an intimate venue or catering for some sort of an event, which could translate into sizeable dollars. At best, he recognized potential when he read about it and wanted to discuss bringing her bistro into their fold.

Since she couldn't get a loan, a partner would be her next best option. Preferably, a silent one who wouldn't interfere with what she'd created and would give her the capital she needed in return for a share of the profits.

A leather portfolio holding her business plan lay on her lap. With a glance at her watch, she let out an uneasy breath. The man was already a half an hour late. As badly as she wanted to talk with him, if he didn't arrive within the next few minutes, she'd have to leave. It was nearly five o'clock. Her bistro reopened at five-thirty for dinner.

Her small waitstaff could dish up the soups du jour she had prepped that morning. In a pinch, they could also help with cold appetizers and salads. But there was no one to prepare the hot appetizers and entrées except Tommi herself. Not since Geoff Ferneau, her brilliant former sous chef, had packed up his knives and left for greener gastronomic pastures three months ago.

Three months and a week, to be precise—which had been a week and a day after he'd charmed his way into her bed following a hugely successful private dinner party and a shared bottle of an excellent Brunello.

She was not, however, going to dwell on what should never have happened with her hired help. Not now. If she did, she'd just start beating herself up all over again for letting herself be seduced by his charm, which was exactly what had happened with the only other man she'd ever been involved with. But she wasn't going to go there now, either. Feeling as protective of her mental energy as she did her physical stamina, she had no desire to waste either on things she couldn't change, anyway.

The fact that her usually endless energy had developed limits lately was why she couldn't wait much longer to hire another chef to help her. One of the caliber she required to maintain the quality of her menu. Because she *had* let herself be seduced, she was now three and a half months pregnant. Without bringing someone onboard soon, she wasn't at all sure how she'd keep up, especially after her baby was born.

Her hand unconsciously slipped to the tiny bulge concealed beneath the stylish jacket of her cocoa-colored suit. She'd spent the first weeks of her pregnancy in denial, and the last couple of months dragging herself out of bed, throwing up, bucking up and, through sheer determination, facing her new reality with an Oscar-worthy portrayal of normalcy. The thought that she carried a baby shook her on a number of levels. So did the knowledge that she would lose customers if she couldn't keep up. If she lost customers, she could lose the restaurant, which meant her staff would lose their jobs—and she would lose the means to support her child.

Even though it had been years since she'd experienced it the first time, the sensation of having the bottom fall out of her world felt all too familiar.

"Tommi Fairchild?"

Her focus had fallen to her lap. Jarred from that disquieting sense of insecurity, it jerked to a pair of large, expensive-looking black loafers planted on the teal and gold carpet.

The leather shoes looked suspiciously Italian—as did the black briefcase carried by the six feet of decidedly gorgeous urban masculinity in a tailored Burberry trench coat and charcoal slacks. Above his crisp white shirt collar, his silver-blue eyes narrowed with unnerving scrutiny on her upturned face.

The hand on her stomach slipped to one side as she straightened. Despite the anxiety she battled, the motion appeared to be nothing more than that of a woman smoothing her jacket.

He definitely wasn't who she was waiting for. Scott was tall and fair and reminded her of the pretty-boy jocks who'd been after her oldest sister in college. The man with a voice as mellow as well-aged brandy easily had the height and lean, athletic build, but his neatly trimmed hair was as dark as midnight, and his arresting features were far too rugged to be considered anything but purely masculine.

An aura of power surrounded him. Or maybe it was control. Or strength. Whatever it was, that quiet command radiated from him like a force field, drawing the glances of other guests and making it impossible for her to shift her own.

An alpha male in a business suit.

"You're waiting for Scott Layman?" he prompted.

It seemed he'd also impaired her ability to speak. With a mental frown for the lapse, she offered a guarded "I am."

"I was afraid you'd left. He tried to call, but the only number he has for you is your work phone. I'm Max Callahan. His business partner."

She hadn't realized his partner was coming, too. Suddenly feeling unprepared, determined to hide it, she smiled and started to lift her hand to shake his. "Mr. Callahan," she said, but he was already moving to the chair angled toward hers.

"It's Max," he corrected. Looking back, his glance skimmed her face, his assessment quick, impersonal, yet completely, unnervingly thorough. From the considering pinch of his broad brow, it seemed clear that he found her to be something other than he'd expected. Less or more, though, she couldn't tell. Nothing in his expression betrayed any hint of his impression of her. "Mind if I sit down?"

"Of course not. Please," she insisted, folding her hands more tightly. She felt totally disadvantaged. This man didn't seem nearly as easygoing as his partner. Certainly, he wasn't prone to Scott's broad smiles. That tempered her own as she glanced across the lobby to see if the man she knew was now there, too.

She wasn't sure if it was the situation in general or Max Callahan himself that had her seeking that nebulous bit of familiarity. She could usually hold her own with just about anyone, particularly on her own turf. She was at her best where she could sauté, flambé, roast, bake or braise and totally in her element with her customers. Yet, the business end of her little establishment put her squarely in the opposite end of her comfort zone. Especially lately.

There was something enormously discouraging about trying to convince a stranger that her bistro could afford to bring in another chef, only to be told that her overhead was too high and her projections weren't realistic before being turned down flatter than a fallen soufflé.

The problem was that Geoff had worked for next to nothing. The replacement she needed to hire would command considerably more than that.

She sat toward the edge of her chair, her legs crossed. Stilling the betraying jiggle of her high-heel-booted foot, she reminded herself that this rather disconcerting man's partner had asked for this meeting.

"Will Scott be here soon?"

Max had set his briefcase beside the chair, tossed his overcoat over the back of it. "As soon as he can be. His conference call was taking longer than he'd expected." A hint of frustration shaded his otherwise casual tone as he hitched at the knees of his slacks and lowered his large frame to the seat. "He asked me to keep you company until he can tie it up."

He sat with his elbows on the chair's arms, the tips of his fingers resting on his powerful thighs, his feet planted wide. Beneath his beautifully tailored suit jacket, his shoulders seemed impossibly wide as he gave her what almost looked like a small smile of apology. Or maybe what made her so aware of his commanding presence was that he didn't seem to occupy the space as much as he did to claim it as his own.

"Keep me company?"

"Actually, what he asked is that I buy you a drink while we wait." One dark eyebrow arched. "I'd be happy to ask a cocktail waitress to serve us here. Unless you'd rather go to the bar."

"Thank you," she replied, confused. She *wasn't* meeting with this man, too? "But a drink isn't necessary."

"Coffee, then? Something else?"

"Really. Nothing. And you don't need to wait with me. Honest," she added, not wanting to sound discourteous. "*Unless you have questions,*" she would have said, realizing he might want to get a feel for the sort of person Layman & Callahan might be dealing with. Except he was already talking.

"Nothing, then." His concession came easily, his inscrutable glance skimming her face once more. "But I'm meeting a client here in a while. Since we're both waiting, we might as well keep each other company until Scott arrives."

It seemed obvious now that she was not meeting with this man, too. That relieved her hugely, though exactly why, she couldn't say. It could have had to do with the faint tension she sensed in him. Something latent and disturbing in its ability to taunt her already knotted nerves. Or, maybe, he was just making her more aware of her own anxiety. "Do you know how long he'll be? I don't mean to sound impatient, but I have to get back to work soon."

"I'd imagine ten minutes or so." At her wince, he added, "Or less."

Max leaned back, intent on ignoring his gnawing frustration with his partner as he openly studied the gracious brunette with the innocent brown eyes. It wasn't her fault that he couldn't get Scott to move faster on the expansion of their own company. And she certainly wasn't responsible for the procrastination that had cost their company the option on the New York office space Max had finally found for them. They needed that office. A branch there would save hours of travel between coasts and allow them to double their business. All Scott had needed to do was sign the papers.

Considering how none of that had anything to do with this woman, it would hardly be fair to be less than civil to her. If he was anything, he was a fair man. At the moment, he was also a little mystified.

Tommi Fairchild was not at all the sort of female who normally piqued Scott Layman's interest. Not by a long shot.

She was attractive enough. Pretty, even, in a quiet, understated sort of way. And young, to his way of thinking, anyway. She was easily a decade younger than his own thirty-eight years. She just didn't possesses any of the other club-scene, arm-candy, tall, leggy blonde characteristics that Scott seemed to prefer.

She wore her shining sable hair skimmed back from her face and twisted to spike up behind her head. Her features were as delicate as a cameo's; her makeup subtle. From what he could tell, she wore little beyond the mascara and shadow that caused her expressive dark eyes to look huge as she again glanced, somewhat uncomfortably, toward the front doors. Her smooth, pale skin almost begged to be touched. Her unadorned mouth looked impossibly soft. Lush. Kissable. And, as her attention returned to him, far too appealing.

With a quick pinch of his brow, he consciously canceled the direction of his thoughts. He felt edgy enough without being reminded of how long he'd been without the intimate company of a woman. As he drew his glance the length of her stylish but conservative slacks and jacket, he allowed himself to consider only what she might mean to his partner. Though he couldn't quite wrap his head around the idea of Scott being so interested in her, his partner had actually insisted that this woman could be the one he "wanted to marry" when he'd asked him to make sure she waited for him.

Not once in the fifteen years he'd worked with the man had he known Scott to be serious about any female for longer than a weekend. But if she could get him to settle down and take his work more seriously than his play, he wasn't about to mess with the course of true love.

Whatever the hell that was.

Despite his own cynicism about the existence of the concept, having the guy take on the responsibilities of a relationship would be the best thing that could happen for Max himself. Because of that, he needed to keep Ms. Fairchild occupied.

"So...where do you work?" he asked, since she'd brought it up.

"The Corner Bistro. I own it," she replied, sounding as if she'd thought he might know that. "The business, anyway. I lease the space." She tipped her head, the soft arches of her eyebrows drawing together. "Scott didn't mention it to you?"

He couldn't imagine why he would have. "The Corner Bistro." He repeated the name, trying to remember if he'd ever heard of the place. A nearly infinite number of eating establishments populated downtown Seattle and its neighborhoods. Some thrived in the highly competitive market. Others came and went with the speed of light. "I'm sorry, but I've been away a lot," he admitted, drawing a blank. "I haven't kept up with restaurants here."

"Only Scott deals in that area of your investments, then?"

"Excuse me?"

"I understand your company is quite diversified," she explained, clearly thrown by his quick frown. "You just said you don't keep up with restaurants, so it sounds as if that must be one of his areas of expertise."

He had no idea what his partner had told this woman, but Scott Layman definitely didn't handle the investment end of their business. The guy could barely manage his personal banking account. "We don't usually invest in restaurants."

"You don't?"

"Not usually," he repeated, and watched her surprise fade to an oddly deflated disappointment.

Doing a commendable job of regrouping, she gave a small shrug and picked at the edge of the smart leather portfolio in her lap. "I guess he must want to talk to me about catering an event, then. If that's the case," she concluded, pondering, "it seems odd that he'd want to meet here instead of at the bistro."

Scott's choice of a high-end hotel with a good bar and impressive rooms hadn't seemed odd at all to Max. At least it hadn't before now. Considering the nature of her comments and the discouragement shadowing her pretty brown eyes, he had the sudden and distinct impression that her reason for being there had nothing to do with his partner's objective.

It seemed she was under the impression she was here for a business meeting. While he and Scott socialized far less than they once had, anything potentially business related was shared. Scott had mentioned nothing to him about any business dealings he might have with her. Everything the guy had said had made it clear he had a date.

"Did he give you reason to think he needed something catered?" he asked, wondering if that was the angle the guy was using to get close to her.

She looked up from her portfolio. "I haven't actually talked to him," she admitted. "Not about why he wanted to see me today, I mean. This meeting was arranged..." With the blink of her dark lashes, she cut herself off. Her eyes, however, remained locked on his. "By a mutual acquaintance," she concluded, then breathed in as if she'd just been sucker-punched.

An awful suspicion lodged hard in Tommi's chest. Until that moment, it hadn't occurred to her that this meeting would be about anything other than her bistro. Probably, she conceded, because protecting it and all it meant to her was so constantly on her mind. According to her mother, the bistro was all she ever thought about, anyway. That was undoubtedly true. It was her life. It just wasn't the life her mother had wanted for her.

"Arranged?"

Her glance fell. "By his secretary."

"Scott's?"

Tommi shook her head, as conscious of Max's eyes narrowing on her as she was of his blunt curiosity. "No. No," she repeated, suddenly wishing she was somewhere, anywhere else. "The other...person's."

Suspicion had just developed a rather mortifying edge.

Her mom had finally come to accept her choice of career. But, as with her other three daughters, she'd been hinting lately at how she wanted Tommi to have a personal life, too. A personal life to Cornelia Fairchild had—also, lately—come to mean marriage and babies. This from the woman Tommi regarded as the queen of independence.

She had no idea what was going on with her mother on that score, but she now had the sick feeling that her mom had mentioned her desire to Uncle Harry. Tommi had always thought of the man her parents had known long before her dad had died as rather eccentric. While he could be amazingly generous at times, he also had a terrible tendency to meddle.

She'd draped her raincoat over the arm of the chair. Mustering as much calm as she could, she picked it up and rose to her feet. Just last month, Harry had attempted to fix up her little sister with a totally-wrong-for-her associate of his. It was because of that misguided mismatch that Bobbie had more or less accosted the man who was now her fiancé, but that was beside the point. Unless she was totally misreading the motives of the man who'd manipulated his own four sons into marriages, Harry had used the review of her restaurant as a ploy to fix her up, too.

Equally humiliating was the possibility that the enviably self-contained and all too disturbing man watching her had realized right along with her that she'd been set up.

"Are you all right?"

"Of course," she hedged, conscious of Max rising as she slipped on her coat. "I'm just late."

With her limited but lousy romantic history, the last thing she wanted right now—make that *ever*—was to get involved with another man. Angry with Harry, angrier with herself for getting her hopes up about help for the bistro when there'd been nothing to get her hopes up for, she picked up her portfolio and reached beside the chair for her shoulder bag.

"I really need to get to work." She tried to smile, trying even harder to appear as if she was only thinking of the time. "We reopen for dinner at five-thirty and I don't have backup."

She'd meant to snag both straps of her bag. Instead, as agitated as she was, she caught only one, and then only its edge. The moment she lifted it, the strap slipped from her fingers and the oversize purse landed sideways on the carpet beside the chair skirt. Her hot pink day planner spilled out, along with a tube of cocoa butter lip gloss, a pen, her checkbook and a stub for the dry cleaning she kept forgetting to pick up.

She could feel heat rising in her cheeks. Embarrassed all over again, she sank to her heels and gathered up the pen and notebook. The lip gloss had rolled to a stop by Max's shoe. Before she could snatch it up, he did.

He'd crouched beside her. A heartbeat later, she felt his fingers curve above her elbow. Yet, instead of helping her up, he held her in place.

"Careful," he said, as if he knew that all she wanted was to spin and run the moment she was upright. "There's a couple walking behind you."

She didn't know which caught her more off guard just then: the gentlemanly gesture and the concern in his hushed tone, or the strong, steadying feel of his hand encircling her arm. There was an unexpected sort of support in his touch, something that felt oddly, inexplicably reassuring. That reassurance was probably only that he wasn't going to let her make a fool of herself by flattening unsuspecting hotel guests, but reassurance in any form was something she needed badly just then.

As he said, "It's okay now," and helped her straighten,

that quiet support also seemed to tell her he wouldn't let go until she had herself together.

The strange calm that came with the thought lasted only long enough for her to murmur, "Thank you," a moment before his hand slipped away.

Still towering beside her, he held out the lip gloss and checkbook he'd retrieved.

His palm was broad, his fingers long. But it was how capable his big hands looked that struck her as she took what he held. Her worldly wise waitress Alaina would say he had hands that would know how to hold a woman.

The fact that she wouldn't mind being held by a man she'd just met simply so she could feel that calm again told her that her stress level must be higher than she'd realized.

"Scott will be disappointed he missed you," he told her, his deep voice as steadying as his grip had been. "But I'll tell him you waited as long as you could."

She couldn't quite meet his eyes. "I appreciate that," she replied, glancing as far as the slight cleft in his chin. Max Callahan was being incredibly gallant, she thought, though the word wasn't one she'd ever applied to a man before. Other than making her aware of how she could still feel heat where his hand had caught her arm, he was doing nothing to make her feel any more self-conscious than she already did. Still, not only was she certain that the meeting with his partner had been a setup, it now also seemed she'd been stood up, too.

"Can I have the valet get your car?"

"I took a cab." With the bistro only a mile away, it had cost less to take a cab than it would have to park in the hotel garage. At the moment, though, she'd gladly pay double not to have to wait for a taxi to get her away from there. "But thank you. And thank you for letting me know why your partner couldn't make it. I hope your client arrives soon."

The faint smile she managed faded even as she turned away.

Max watched her go, more intrigued than he wanted to be by the number of emotions he'd seen cross the delicate lines of her face. There was an artlessness about her that spoke of sincerity, and she possessed no artifice at all. The women he'd known over the years were far more practiced at masking little things like awkwardness and embarrassment, and while she'd done a commendable job of maintaining her composure, there was no doubt in his mind that she'd felt both. He'd seen them in her profile as she'd snatched up her belongings, sensed them even more profoundly when he'd caught her arm to slow her down.

What he'd been aware of most, though, was how she'd almost unconsciously drawn toward him in the moments he'd held her there, and the totally unfamiliar sense of protectiveness he'd felt when she had.

Now, as then, he dismissed the feeling as an aberration. If he'd felt protective about anything, it was only of his partner's interest in her. She wasn't the sort of woman he'd be interested in himself, anyway—had he been looking for one.

He liked sophisticated, worldly women who'd experienced enough of life to not have expectations they couldn't realize on their own. He preferred a woman who knew the rules, who didn't expect him to bail her out of her latest crisis and who had no illusions about romance, being rescued by a knight in shining armor, living happily ever after, or whatever all it was some women called "the fairy tale." He was nobody's prince. The only thing he was interested in rescuing was the lease his partner had let lapse. As for living happily ever after, if Scott wanted to entertain the myth, that was fine with him.

He just wasn't interested himself. His own short foray into wedded bliss a lifetime ago had been an unmitigated disaster. As for family, a man couldn't miss what he'd never really had. He was doing just fine without encumbrances that would only slow him down, anyway.

He turned back to the chair, vaguely aware of conversations beyond him in the elegant lobby, but conscious mostly of the need to move to the next item on his agenda. He'd told his client and longtime sailing buddy, J. T. Hunt, that he'd meet him in the bar.

He had his coat over one arm and had reached for his briefcase when he noticed a slash of bright pink under the skirt of the chair beside him.

Crouching down, he pulled out a small wallet. It was the same bright color as the day planner Tommi had snatched up.

He flipped the wallet open, glanced at the driver's license. The Department of Motor Vehicles photograph didn't begin to do justice to her features, but he'd have recognized the intriguing woman in it even if her name hadn't been right there.

She just wasn't anywhere in sight when he reached the street to give it back to her.

Pocketing the wallet to give to Scott to return to her, he headed back inside. It was just as well she'd already gone, he thought. Out of sight meant out of mind.

She just wasn't out of sight for long.

Chapter Two

"I'm taking the last of the crab bisque, Tommi. The other order's for the ragout."

Tommi looked from the pan of scallops she was sautéing. Shelby Hahn had clipped another ticket to the order wheel on her way to the stock pots. Her burgundy-tipped black hair stood in short gelled spikes around her narrow face. Narrower black glasses framed blue eyes made violet by the grape shadow covering her lids. The most demure thing about the bubbly young waitress and part-time spin-class instructor was her uniform. On her, the black blouse and slacks and short red bistro apron looked positively sedate.

Tommi gave the pan a shake, causing flame to surge from the gas burner of the big commercial stove as butter and olive oil splattered. Overhead, the exhaust hood droned. With her thoughts bouncing between her orders and her current situation, she barely noticed the familiar white noise. On her good news/bad news scale, she was even for the day so far. The third bank had called that morning, turning her down and making the uncertainty she was living with loom that much larger.

On the upside, she'd once again managed to make it through her morning queasiness before anyone else had shown up. According to the mother-to-be sites she'd checked on the internet, the problem should be tapering off soon—right about the time it would become next to impossible to hide the more visible signs of impending motherhood.

She wasn't going to dwell on that. For now, she'd just be grateful her pregnancy wasn't noticeable and that she'd been spared morning sickness in the afternoon and evenings, too. As she pressed the sleeve of her white chef's jacket to her upper lip, she just hoped that the kitchen's heat wouldn't bring the sensation back before she could step outside for a break. In a pinch, she'd learned that she could always slip into the freezer. Cold helped. Enormously.

"We're down to two, maybe three orders on the ragout," she said to Shelby, mentally calculating the orders that had come in for it. Running low on specials was another reason to hope the lunch rush was easing. "How are we doing out there?"

"There's no one waiting to be seated," the waitress replied, dishing up bisque, "and some of the tables have cleared. Oh, and the guy who ordered the ragout wants to know when you'll have the rustic mushroom soup on the menu again."

As soon as I can stand the smell of raw garlic in the morning, Tommi told herself.

"Is that Ernie? From the copy place?" she asked, thinking of the balding customer who ate there every other Tuesday. He loved her rustic mushroom.

"It's not him. This guy said his broker told him he needed to try it."

God bless word of mouth, Tommi thought. "Tell him I'll make it next week. Friday," she decided, praying that by then she could handle the bulb's pungent scent. "And thank him for asking."

"Will do."

Behind her, the long shelf below the plating station held stacks of white dishes. A square plate mounded with fresh mixed greens sat on its stainless-steel surface. Turning with pan and tongs in hand, she arranged the seared scallops atop the leaf lettuce and escarole. Adding a drizzle of honey-chipotle vinaigrette and two oval parmesan crisps, she moved the garnished dish to the end of the station.

Tommi had just ladled wild mushroom and beef ragout into a boule of warm country bread and handed it to Shelby to serve to the table with the bisque when Alaina Morretti came through the swinging door.

The older waitress wasn't carrying an order ticket. With a relieved smile for that, Tommi flipped off the burner and stepped to the triple sink on the back wall. Anyone watching would think she was just rinsing her hands. Mostly, she was letting the cold water splash against her wrists.

"There's a man asking for you. A seriously gorgeous man," Alaina pronounced. With a hand on one rounded hip, her other rested at the base of her throat. Above her fingertips winked the silver Best Soccer Mom necklace her kids had given her for her last birthday. "We're talking Michelangelo quality here. Carved, sculpted. And that's just his face. I'm betting there's some major muscle going on under all that Armani."

The divorced mother of three had sworn off men herself. At least until her demanding brood was grown and she found the time and the nerve to put herself out there again.

A short series of even shorter relationships had left her totally gun-shy. That didn't stop her from looking, though. "He wants to see you when you have a minute."

Tommi pulled a paper towel from its dispenser. Beneath the short white chef's toque covering her hair, one eyebrow shot up. "Is he a customer?"

"I've never seen him here before. He just walked in and asked for you."

Drying her hands, Tommi headed for the door and peeked out the small square window on the side marked "out." Her glance darted past the wine bar where two gentlemen visited on tall black stools and past the short rows of tables lining her cozy bistro's old brick walls. Several of her seven white-clothed tables for two were still full, as were the two four-tops in the middle of the narrow room. The rest had already been reset with utensils and a tumbler sporting a red napkin that had been rolled, folded and tucked inside.

"He said his name is Max Callahan."

Even before she heard his name, Tommi's focus had landed on the tall, dark and disturbing man in the black overcoat talking on his cell phone by the hostess desk. At several of the tables—those occupied by females, anyway—heads leaned together as whispers were exchanged. Max didn't seem to notice the attention he drew. His only interest seemed to be in his call and the time as he glanced at his watch and turned away as if to keep his conversation private.

Tommi almost groaned—would have had the clearly curious Alaina not now been at her elbow. She'd spent a lot of time lately trying to find something positive about bad situations. There were times when she'd had to dig really deep for that bright spot. And finding something even remotely encouraging about her embarrassing non-meeting with Scott Layman had been a greater challenge than most. Especially the part where his partner had witnessed that humiliation.

Apparently, she wasn't even going to be allowed the little silver lining she'd finally found. The only good thing she'd come up with about yesterday's fiasco was knowing she'd never have to see Max Callahan again.

Now looking out the window herself, the older woman leaned closer. "Is he the one who sent the flowers?"

The huge bouquet of red roses near the far end of the wine bar had been delivered midmorning. After reading the card that had come with it, Tommi had felt embarrassed all over again by Scott's seemingly sincere apology for having left her waiting. She'd also left the bouquet out front. Keeping it in her office made the gift seemed too personal. Besides, the crimson blooms were the closest thing she had to Christmas decor at the moment. Though every other commercial establishment in town had had their holiday decorations up for what seemed like weeks, she hadn't been able to get into the holiday frame of mind enough to even hang a wreath.

Her only comment to her staff about the sender had been that he was a businessman who'd sent them in apology for having to miss an appointment.

"No. No, he's not," she said, killing her waitress's speculation. She had no idea what Max was doing here. She just knew she didn't want to see him out front while she still had customers. "Show him to the kitchen, will you, please?"

Rainwater dripped from Max's open overcoat as he ended the call from his secretary. Facing the wet street from the dry side of the glass door, he distractedly snapped his cell phone onto his belt clip. It wasn't raining hard outside, but he'd had to park a block down from the five-story, redbrick building where Tommi's establishment anchored one corner. Between the curved green awning over the brass and glass door and the way she'd had The Corner Bistro stenciled in gold on both large windows, the place had been easy enough to find.

He'd have taken off his coat had he thought he'd be there long, but he'd only come by to do what his partner hadn't had time to do himself before Scott had left for Singapore.

The fact that Scott had forgotten to mention that he was leaving two days early was just one more straw in the haystack of frustrations that had accompanied Max inside. Scott's secretary had assumed Scott had talked to him about the change he'd had her make. Margie Higgins, Max's assistant, had thought the same. Max had actually learned of the earlier departure purely by coincidence from J. T. Hunt last night.

J.T. had been HuntCom's chief architect before he'd left his father's multibillion-dollar computer company a while back and gone into business for himself. Aside from the consulting work Max had done over the years with him and his brother Gray, HuntCom's CEO, he and J.T. shared a mutual interest in sailing. That interest had prompted last evening's meeting. J.T. wanted to sell his sloop to buy a bigger one for his growing family. Max had introduced him to a client interested in buying it. Conversation had inevitably turned to their respective businesses, though. That was when J.T. had innocuously asked about the expansion sites Gray was meeting Scott in Singapore tomorrow to see.

Max knew Scott tended to be pretty laid-back at times, but it wasn't like him to forget something as basic as keeping him in the loop with a major client. Scott was a smart man. He knew it took teamwork to juggle projects of the size they constantly dealt with.

Just as he knew how hard it was to get prime Upper East Side office space.

For months, Scott had been totally onboard with the idea of opening a New York office. He had even said he'd be willing to relocate there himself. He would handle the clients and accounts in the East. Max would do the same with the West. They'd split responsibilities at their Chicago branch. All they had to do was move some experienced staff from Chicago and Seattle to work in New York, hire the best of the best as they always did to fill in the gaps in all three places and they'd be up and running.

Except, now, they didn't have an office—which meant Max needed to look for another one.

With irritation climbing up his back over that little addition to his already crowded agenda, Max tried hard to imagine what was going on with his partner. The only reason he could come up with for Scott's lapse—and for his failure to mention his change in plans—was the guy's uncharacteristic preoccupation with Tommi Fairchild.

"Mr. Callahan?"

At the sound of his name, he turned to the middle-aged waitress with the short chop of blond-on-blond hair. Like the younger waitress with the even shorter hair in shades that reminded him of a bruise, her long-sleeved black blouse and slacks looked as crisp and sharp as the smooth red apron tied low at her waist. He liked their look. It was at once trendy and professional. Their boss had good taste.

"Tommi will see you in the back. Come with me, please."

With a pleasant smile, she turned for him to follow. It

was only as he did that his preoccupation faded enough to appreciate the surprisingly cozy, urban yet rustic space.

He'd noticed the framed reviews on the wall by the hostess desk, and been vaguely aware of the constant murmur of the patrons' conversations. What he noted now were the two huge paintings of wine bottles in reds, burgundies and shades of slate hanging on one of the tall brick walls. Like the mural painted over the boarded-up window in the storefront next door, those same colors slashed across an equally sizeable abstract on the opposite wall of white.

Conscious of his large frame, he moved along a narrow aisle formed between the occupied tables. As he did, he became even more aware of the mouthwatering aromas that had reminded him when he'd walked in that he needed lunch.

Since he'd been on the phone with Margie at the time, and knowing he had a 1:30 conference call, he'd already asked his secretary to order him a sandwich to eat at his desk. Noticing a freshly delivered, rather incredible-looking panini in front of a guy at the wine bar and the size of the shrimp on a plate of pasta by his companion, he thought now he should have just ordered to-go from here.

The blonde waitress held open the right side of a pair of narrow swinging doors.

Murmuring his thanks, he stepped past her, reached inside his overcoat pocket and walked into the small, efficient space.

The room behind him offered texture, comfort and warmth. Here, stainless steel seemed to be the surface of choice. Racks, pots, pans, appliances. Much of it bore the patina of wear. Some shone with a glint that spoke of more recent purchase. All of it looked scrupulously organized. What had the bulk of his attention, though, was the unease in the features of the woman he'd met yesterday as she turned from setting a pan in a long, deep sink.

The white double-breasted chef's jacket Tommi Fairchild wore over loose black pants was buttoned to her throat. A short white toque covered her head. Even with her hair hidden, he remembered its shine and its color. That rich warm brown held the same shades of gold as the flecks in her dark and wary eyes.

He had no idea why he remembered those details. Especially since he wasn't close enough to note much about her eyes other than the caution clouding them when she offered a small smile.

"Hi," she said, walking toward him as she wiped her hands on the apron tied at her waist. Looking as hesitant as she sounded, she stopped ten feet away. "What brings you here?"

He knew she'd been embarrassed yesterday. Beyond embarrassed, probably, considering how totally she'd misconstrued the reason for his partner's interest in her. There seemed to be another element to her discomfort now, though.

From her puzzled question, she clearly hadn't expected him.

"Didn't Scott call you?"

"He called this morning," she confirmed, looking as if she wasn't at all sure what that had to do with his presence. "He apologized for not being able to meet yesterday."

"But he didn't say anything about what you'd left at the hotel."

He offered the conclusion flatly, burying the exasperation that came with it as he took a step closer. Scott had offered no explanation for yesterday's misunderstanding with this woman when he'd called on his way to the airport. Not that Max had wanted, or asked for one. Realizing last night that he couldn't give the wallet to Scott to give to this woman himself since Scott wouldn't be around, all Max had asked was that Scott let her know he had it and that he'd get it to her sometime that day.

So much for follow-through.

"You dropped this," he told her, and held out the small rectangle of hot pink leather he'd pulled from his pocket. "It fell out of your bag."

There was no need to mention when it had fallen out. The unease in her expression told him there wasn't much about yesterday that she'd managed to forget. Still, surprise stole much of that discomfort the instant she'd noticed what he held. It also had her speaking in a rush, making one word out of three.

"Ohmygosh. I didn't even realize it was gone!"

"I thought you'd have missed it when you went to pay for your cab."

"I had money in my coat pocket. Change from the ride over," she explained, stepping closer to take her wallet from him. "I had no idea it had fallen out, too." Apparently realizing she was repeating herself, or maybe just not wanting to think about how desperately she'd wanted to leave the hotel, she cut herself off, shook her head. "Thank you," she murmured as the door behind them swung open. "Thank you very much."

The younger waitress with short, spiked hair breezed in carrying an empty bread basket. As she headed for a tray of baguettes, Tommi turned into a short hall separating an open doorway from a wall of dry goods.

"And thank your partner, too, please," she continued, her hushed voice encouraging him to follow, "for the roses he sent. It was kind of him, but it really wasn't necessary. What happened yesterday wasn't entirely his fault," she insisted, backing into a closet-sized office. "The miscommunication about why we were meeting, I mean. I'm sure he'd been misinformed somehow on his end, too."

Behind her, the wall was filled by a tall bookcase crammed with cookbooks and cooking magazines. A red metal desk and two black filing cabinets took up the narrow wall beside her. The top of one held binders, files and a gym bag. The other served as a space for culinary trophies that looked stored there rather than displayed. On the neatly arranged desk, below a bulletin board feathered with a haphazard array of wedding, birth and graduation announcements half covered by notes and reminders, a computer shared space with invoices and hand-written recipe notes.

She opened the desk's bottom drawer and bent to drop in her wallet. As she did, he couldn't help but wonder at the odd mix of disarray and organization in the cramped and crowded space. It seemed as if she tried to control the chaos with order, but just couldn't quite succeed. What struck him most, though, was her easy sense of fairness. Or maybe it was forgiveness.

He didn't know many women who wouldn't have thought flowers the least a guy could offer after leaving her sitting so long. But she still didn't seem to be on the same wavelength as his partner, either. However the meeting had come about, which he considered no business of his, Scott's personal interest in her remained unquestionable. He'd even made a point of asking Max to say only nice things about him, and to tell her he'd make up for the misunderstanding as soon as he got back next week.

I'm not asking you to sell me, buddy, he'd said, *but at least don't say anything that'll scare her off. Okay? I'd be a fool to let her get away.*

The guy had it bad. Which was fine with Max. As sensible as Tommi sounded, she'd probably be good for him.

Still, he wasn't comfortable at all playing messenger between his colleague and the man's intended romantic target. If Scott wanted her to know he'd make up for having pretty much stood her up, he could tell her that himself. If she wanted Scott to know he didn't need to send roses, ditto. He was still curious, though, about the disappointment underlying her consternation yesterday when she'd figured out that the meeting hadn't been about business.

"Miscommunication," he repeated as she nudged the drawer closed. "It's pretty obvious now that Scott thought he had a date with you. Do you mind if I ask why you thought you were meeting him?"

The hint of disquiet in her expression belied the dismissal in her small shrug. "I thought he wanted to talk about my bistro."

"What made you think that?"

"Because I was told that he'd read my latest review and wanted to meet me."

"Do you always meet men who read your reviews?"

She eyed him evenly. "I do when the man is an investor and I'm in need of one. I saw on your website that Layman & Callahan invests in local businesses. I'd hoped to talk to him about mine." A regretful little smile curved her mouth. "But that was before you said your company doesn't invest in restaurants."

"What I said," he clarified, conscious of her lingering disappointment, "is that we *usually* don't. Our investors expect a certain return on their money. A business has to be big enough to produce an assured annual revenue before we'll look at it."

She frowned at that.

"What made you think mine wasn't big enough?"

"The Corner Bistro?"

She'd named her place exactly what it was. And what it was, was small.

"Oh," she murmured, and went silent.

His own quick silence had more to do with the deafening sound of opportunity knocking.

He had no idea how Scott intended to pursue this establishment's admittedly intriguing owner. All he knew for certain was that it could be in his own best interests if the guy succeeded, and that the opportunity to help both himself and his partner was literally staring him in the face.

In the years since he'd helped the former college football hero save the company Scott had inherited from his father, Max had taken the business that did the legwork for corporations looking to relocate, from regional to national and beyond. As agreed when Max had achieved what Scott had thought impossible, Layman & Son had become Layman & Callahan. Driven, focused and refusing to stop there, Max had grown the company to include property investments for the same corporate officers who sought them for their company's expansions.

Tommi Fairchild's bistro was definitely smaller than the apartment buildings, hotels, trendy nightclubs and high-end restaurants in their partnership portfolio. But the place did have potential. The framed reviews by the hostess desk were four-star. Aside from the FedEx guy eating a bowl of soup and two women with Book Nook shopping bags, the customers he'd seen leaving by cab and under umbrellas appeared to be brokers, secretaries celebrating someone's birthday, and attorney-types from the high rises a mile away. To bring people out in the rain in the middle of the work week, it seemed to him that her food and service must be pretty amazing.

He wouldn't play messenger, but as he watched Tommi Fairchild's pretty brown eyes shift toward the doorway as if waiting for him to move, he could certainly start checking out the place as a possible investment. Since working with her would give Scott the perfect excuse to hang around, his partner could pick up the ball when he got back and take it from there.

"You said yesterday that you own this," he reminded her, not above doing whatever he had to do to achieve a goal. As long as it was legal, anyway. "Are you the sole proprietor?"

Looking surprised by the question, or maybe surprised that he remembered what she'd said, her glance shifted back to him. "I am."

He'd wondered before how that was possible, given how young she appeared. He wondered again now. "Do you mind telling me what kind of financing you have?"

"I have a small SBA loan," she said, speaking of the Small Business Administration. "I needed it to buy a salamander and add the wine bar."

"Salamander?"

"It's a kind of broiler. I use it for fish and to melt and brown cheese on onion soup, and to caramelize the sugar and cook the fruit for some of my salads. The pear carpaccio, especially."

"That's it?"

"Oh, not at all." Enthusiasm brightened her eyes as she quickly shook her head. "It's good for crisping toppings, too, or to bring the temperature up on a dish that had to wait while others for a table were prepared. It's a great piece of equipment. If I need to deepen a glaze—"

"I meant," he said, patiently he hoped, "that's it as far as who's financially involved in the business."

Her quick zeal faded with her quiet. "Oh. That's it, then."

"There's no bank? No investor?"

She shook her head.

"No loan from a boyfriend?"

"No," she said flatly.

"How about friends?" he ventured, noting the unquestionable finality in her last response. "Any side loans you have to repay for getting started? Any family members you owe?"

"I understand what you mean by financially involved," she informed him, her expression graciously tolerant. "But I said there's no one. As for my family, they didn't want me becoming a chef in the first place. Mom and two of my sisters, anyway. This is all mine."

The admissions caught him a little off guard. Especially the claim about her family. She didn't strike him as much of a rebel. But instead of being intrigued by the possibility, or asking why her family had been against something that appeared so successful, he made himself focus on the note of protective ownership in her voice. Given how proprietary owners could be about what they'd created, that attitude could be a problem in a partnership. But that was the analytical part of him.

Another part, the purely male part, had settled on her mouth.

As yesterday, that gentle fullness remained unadorned. There was no gloss or shine to interfere with its texture, the ripe-peach blush of its color, its taste.

Now, as then, he couldn't help but wonder if it would feel as soft as it looked.

A muscle in his jaw jerked.

"What do you want an investor for?"

Aware of his scrutiny, more aware of his faint frown, Tommi felt the same sense of disadvantage she had when she'd first met him. It was as if he knew something about her that she didn't, and he wasn't sharing. Or maybe what brought the vaguely intimidating feeling was the way his big body had her more or less trapped in her office.

She wasn't accustomed to feeling intimidated. Or to being so conscious of a man.

But she wasn't accustomed to being pregnant, either. Or to needing help. Or to craving the odd reassurance she'd felt from him yesterday and would give just about anything in the world to feel again.

Even as she scrambled to deny that unwanted admission, she couldn't help the hope that flickered.

"I need to hire a sous chef." She'd bet her best sauté pan that he was not a person who wasted time. Especially his own. If he was asking questions, it was for a reason. "When I opened two years ago, I only served breakfast and lunch.

"Six months ago," she continued, telling him exactly what she'd told all the loan officers who'd turned her down, "I hired a sous chef for next to nothing and started staying open for dinner. He left for an opportunity he couldn't refuse," she told him, sweeping past enough details to choke a goat. "Since then, I've been through two experienced cooks and a trainee, but none of them fit with what we have here. The person I want requires more in the way of salary than I paid Geoff, but he's exactly who I need to maintain the quality and feel of my kitchen."

"Why'd the other guy work for so little?"

"Because he was just looking for experience," she said, which was exactly what she'd known when she'd hired him.

"And this other chef?"

"We went to culinary school together. He's working in San Francisco right now, but he's moving back to Seattle in February," she explained quickly. "He's been offered another position here, but he hasn't accepted it yet. He'll work for me if I can match their offer. He just can't afford a cut in pay. He has a family to support."

The man blocking most of her doorway remained silent as his sharp blue eyes moved over her face. She had no idea what conclusions he might be drawing about anything she'd just said. She couldn't even tell if she'd piqued his interest or killed it. His beautifully carved and annoyingly guarded features gave away absolutely nothing.

Neither did his tone.

"I should let you get back to work," he finally said. He glanced at his watch, something that flashed platinum and probably cost as much as the salary she was hoping to cover. "I need to get going myself. I'll take a look at your books, if you're still interested in showing them to us. Scott won't be back for a week, but it's me you'd deal with initially, anyway."

Tommi felt herself go still. She blinked, breathed in. Just like that. He wanted to look at her books.

"Of course I'm interested." Fighting the urge to hug him, amazed by how badly she wanted to do just that, she looked behind her, looked back. "Hang on just a sec."

Max could almost swear he felt her relief. That he could sense what this woman felt so distinctly would have bothered him, too, had he considered the odd phenomenon. Sensitivity had never been his strong suit. Or so he'd been told by his ex, and a few other women who'd wanted to get closer than he cared to allow. As it was, he just wondered why she felt that relief so strongly. He could have understood her reaction had she been drowning in debt or facing foreclosure, but all she wanted was to hire a chef.

Or so he was thinking when he watched her turn from the drawer she'd just opened. As she faced him with the portfolio she'd had with her yesterday, she was smiling. Not with the restraint he'd seen before, but with an ease that lit the little chips of gold in her dark eyes. That same ease relieved the strain he hadn't even noticed until that stress no longer tensed the fragile lines of her face.

Sunshine, he thought. She had a smile like sunshine. Warm. Renewing.

Healing.

That warmth seemed to touch something deep inside him. Something buried in a place he hadn't even realized existed until he felt the tension inside himself easing, too. He'd lived with that restiveness for so long it had become as familiar as breathing.

The unexpected thoughts came out of nowhere. Much like the unfamiliar need he'd felt to shield her from adding to her embarrassment at the hotel yesterday.

He wasn't at all sure what to make of her effect on him. He did know, though, that he had no business letting her affect him at all.

She'd removed a manila envelope from the portfolio. "These are copies of my profit and loss statements and projections for next year. It's what the banks said they needed, but if you need anything else, I'll get a copy to you as soon as I can."

He took what she held, a faint edge entering his voice. "You've been trying to get a loan."

"Trying," she admitted, suddenly cautious, though from his question or his tone, he couldn't tell.

"I'm not promising we can do business, either," he warned. If he couldn't legitimately justify a partnership, Scott could always steer her in another direction, if that was what he wanted to do. For now, all he wanted himself was to make sure the lines between her and Scott stayed open. "You should know that being vetted for a partnership doesn't work quite the same way as applying for a loan.

"This is good," he said, holding up the envelope, "but I'll

need to go over your books. I'll need to look around here, too." There'd be inventory to verify, employees to discuss, possible changes to go over before commitments could be made. If they were made at all. "When is a good time for that?"

"Between two-thirty and five-thirty. That's when I'm closed to do the final prep for dinner or run errands if I have to," she explained, wondering if it was her quick tension she felt. Or his. "My staff is almost always gone by three and comes back about five."

Aware of movement in the kitchen, her voice dropped. "I'd really rather no one knows what all is going on until I have everything in place. It's bad for morale if staff thinks there's a financial problem."

There was also the matter of her sisters. Since a couple of them tended to drop by unannounced, if her chatty staff knew what she was looking into, then her family might eventually hear. Her family would then want to know why she was sacrificing her financial independence and she'd have to tell them about the baby. She was nowhere near ready for that.

"Or Monday evening," she added, more than willing to accommodate. "I'm closed then. And Sunday."

Beneath the dark, windblown hair tumbling over his brow, Max's heavy eyebrows merged. "What do you mean, what 'all' is going on? I can understand keeping financial arrangements private, but don't they already know you're hiring another chef?"

"Of course they do," she assured him. They'd suffered through the other cooks right along with her. "I just…" She hesitated, scrambling to think of a graceful way to get past the totally unintended slip of her tongue. "I just have some personal things going on," she admitted, minimizing hugely. "Nothing that will affect what you're doing," she concluded. "Honest."

He wasn't sure he believed that. "Personal things" had a way of affecting everything else, which was why he kept his personal life limited to whatever helped him in business.

Behind him, quick footsteps came to a halt.

"Sorry, Tommi," he heard the younger waitress say, "but you have an onion soup, two scallops and a panini."

"Thanks, Shelby. I'm on my way."

"I'll call you," he said, stepping back as footsteps hurried off.

Her response was to hit him with that smile again as the other waitress came through, talking about someone out front who wanted to see her about booking a Christmas party for twenty on the ninth.

When he walked out, he could hear her telling the waitress they already had a party booked on that date, but that she'd talk to the customer herself. What he told himself was to stop wondering if she was still smiling and to focus on the questions she'd already raised about her business.

He could have staffed out all those queries. Most, he did. A couple, he looked into himself. But between what he found and the report that came back to him from L&C's data collection section, what he learned about the appealing Ms. Fairchild elicited far more questions than answers.

Chapter Three

In the two days since Max Callahan had walked out of Tommi's kitchen, she'd tried hard not to dwell on what he might be thinking of her little operation. The prospects were just too discouraging. Now that she'd had time to consider just how big Layman & Callahan was, she had the feeling she was seriously out of their league when it came to investments.

Mostly, she'd considered Max himself.

She knew successful men. She knew handsome men. She knew wealthy players and sharks and the sort of guys who could sweep a girl off her feet, then walk away without a backward glance—the latter, from personal experience. The rest she'd grown up knowing, encountered in her mother's and Uncle Harry's social circles or rubbed elbows with working in upscale restaurants over the years. They were also the sort of men her older sisters tended to attract. But Max seemed to be in a league of his own—a combination of all of the above. And the future of nearly everything she cared about rested in his very capable-looking hands.

With him due to arrive in minutes to go over her books, his hands were something she tried not to think about as she pulled a rack of steaming plates from the dishwasher and pushed in the next load. Thinking about them reminded her of what she'd felt when he'd touched her. The moment had been fleeting, less than a minute out of that whole awkward encounter the day she'd first met him. Yet, no matter how she'd tried to deny it, the need for the reassurance she'd felt at that contact still lingered. So had the unfamiliar, oddly threatening yearning he had aroused.

The quiet sense of discipline about him spoke of a man accustomed to responsibility, of someone in control of himself and everything around him. The easy confidence he exuded made it seem as if he could handle anything thrown in his path. Then, there was that quiet sense of strength that made a woman fantasize about leaning on him, letting him bear her burdens for her. Or, at the least, taking them away long enough for her to adjust to their weight.

Not, she reminded herself as she added soap and lowered the washer's hood, that he had given her any indication whatsoever that he'd be inclined to allow such a possibility. And not that she had any intention of leaning on him or any other man. Despite her mother's murmurings of late about seeing her daughters "settled," Cornelia Fairchild had raised all four of her girls to stand on their own, to deal with whatever came up and move on.

That, and to be financially independent.

There had been a time when Tommi probably wouldn't have had to worry about money at all. Her father had been their Uncle Harry's business partner and part owner of HuntCom, the computer company that had become the industry's giant. When her father had died a little over eighteen years ago, the company hadn't been near the size it was now, but it had already been worth millions. They'd lived in a beautiful neighborhood, in a beautiful home. Tommi and her sisters had attended private schools with other children of privilege. They'd traveled, had a cook and a housekeeper and had truly lacked for nothing.

Unlike Harry Hunt, who happened to be brilliant when it came to computers but who treated his own sons with the compassion of a silicon chip, George Fairchild had been an affable, involved father who'd doted on his girls and their mom. Tommi had adored him. He hadn't seemed to mind that she wasn't as athletic and outgoing as Bobbie, as witty and cerebral as Frankie or as striking and musically gifted as Georgie. She'd been the quiet one—not shy so much as simply content to stay in the background, or hang out in the kitchen with the cook. Her dad had loved her brownies. Even the dry ones. Or so he'd said.

He'd been her knight in shining armor, her hero, the center of her universe. When an unexpected heart attack had taken him when Tommi was ten years old, she'd been devastated.

They all had been. But they hadn't just lost a husband and father. No one had known until then that George Fairchild had a gambling problem. He'd owned half of HuntCom, but he'd used most of his share of the company's stock to secure loans to support his habit. He'd mortgaged the house to the hilt, gambled away money he should have used to pay life insurance premiums, which meant there'd been little insurance at all, and left a mountain of gaming debt.

There were details Tommi hadn't been privy to; things her mother had chosen to spare her and her sisters and never shared in the aftermath of that shattering discovery. Though their mom had somehow made sure they stayed in the same good schools, all Tommi had really known at the time was that they'd had to move from their lovely home, that their housekeeper and cook hadn't gone with them and that their mother had spent years paying off those obligations. Except to pay for school trips, she'd absolutely refused Uncle Harry's help. Her husband had created the mess, so she would clean it up. She would not rely on Harry's charity.

Tommi hadn't known if it had been pride or something more nebulous that had guided her mother back then. For all she knew, it might well have been self-preservation. After all, having placed all her faith in one man only to have him let her down so badly, it made sense that she wouldn't want to count on another. Or maybe what she hadn't wanted was whatever obligation Harry's help might have created.

It had been a lesson learned, though. One Tommi had taken to heart. If a woman didn't rely on a man, he couldn't let her down. Even after all these years, she remembered how lost she'd felt without her father and the awful uncertainty she'd grown up with, having had her sense of security so thoroughly shaken.

She couldn't remember exactly when she'd decided she would do whatever it took to get that sense of security back. She just knew she'd also promised herself that, once she had, she would never put herself in a position to feel that way again.

Yet, it was security that was missing from her life now, and what she needed badly to restore. For herself. For her child. The little life growing inside her at that very moment depended on her to make the right choices for her future. Her. It would be a girl. She felt that as surely as she did the need to at least pretend to be as strong as her mother had been back then.

It was the least of what her mother would expect of her now.

With that thought pushing her, she moved to her next task and opened one of the ovens to check the progress of her cassoulet. Breaking the crust, she ladled its broth over the mélange of meats and white beans. The motions were routine, and comforting in their familiarity. In her kitchen, she felt confident, capable. She had her father to thank for that. Cooking had become her escape from the awful pain of life without him all those years ago, as well as a way to contribute to her family's care. It was not knowing if the partnership she needed would actually materialize that made it feel as if the rest of the floor just waited to be pulled out from under her.

Then there was Max himself: The fact that he had her feeling so off balance didn't help at all.

The ladle clattered against the side of the pan. She didn't want the thoughts he provoked; that unfamiliar and persistent need to be assured that everything would be all right. It was up to her to make things okay. No one else. As for the need to be held, she'd chalk that up to hormones, pretty much the way she had her craving for the sugary, dry cereal that kept her nausea at bay in the mornings.

She couldn't believe she was actually eating the empty-carb-loaded stuff, much less eating it straight from its cartoon packaging. But she could use a handful of her hidden stash now.

The security camera above her back door sent images to the small monitor near the kitchen's wall clock. As the buzzer by the door's frame sounded and her glance darted to the screen, she just wasn't sure if the queasy feeling in the pit of her stomach had been brought on by the heat of the dishwasher and oven or because her potential savior had just jump-started those touchy nerves.

Max's secretary had said he'd be there at three-fifteen. The man was nothing if not punctual.

"Come on in," she called, pushing the heavy pan back into the heat.

With all in her kitchen under control for the moment, she rested her hand over the uneasy sensation in her stomach and tossed the hot pads onto the prep station. She didn't have time to get to her Puff Pops. Hearing the solid thud of male footsteps coming through the alleyway door, she opted for the rescue she used when others were around and made a quick dash into her small walk-in refrigerator.

There, between a rack of eggs and dairy on one side and fresh-that-morning Dungeness crabs and halibut steaks on the other, she unbuttoned the top buttons of her chef's jacket and peeled back the layers of fabric to let the cold air hit her upper chest. The double-breasted garment was designed to cover a cook well enough to keep hot, spattering liquids from reaching flesh and burning, and also to button the opposite way so the fabric always appeared clean, but lately, all that material could feel awfully warm.

Even as the blessedly cold air cooled her skin and filled her lungs, she realized the sensation in her stomach now seemed mostly like knotted nerves.

Slowly breathing out, insisting to herself that it was the situation causing the anxiety and not the man she was about to see, she stepped from the chilly space prepared to offer him a business-like hello and a cup of coffee.

Her glance had barely moved from the broad shoulders of his trench coat to the carved lines of his profile when her greeting froze. Max had stopped not far from where the dishwasher quietly sloshed and steamed through its cycle. Rather than facing into the kitchen and looking for her, he aimed a scowl in the direction he'd come.

He must have sensed her there.

With his dark eyebrows drawn into a slash, his narrowed glance darted from the back door to where she'd emerged from behind one of stainless steel. The charcoal color of his coat deepened the quicksilver blue of his eyes. The sight of her seemed to deepen his frown.

"What's wrong?" she asked.

He looked from the knot of hair on her head to the deep vee of skin she'd exposed below her collarbone. The fuller feminine cleavage she'd recently developed seemed to catch his glance, holding it long enough to cause her heart to bump hard against her ribs.

Having quite effectively quickened her pulse, his eyebrows tightened an instant before his focus flicked to her face.

"Do you always leave the back door unlocked?"

Conscious of where his eyes had touched, just as aware of his inexplicable displeasure, she nudged one side of her lapel a bit higher. "Only when the front door is bolted and I'm expecting someone back here."

"You should rethink that. That alley is pretty secluded. Anyone could have walked in," he informed her, his attention fixed firmly on her face. "There were two derelicts out there just now, hanging around the Dumpster."

She'd thought before that he wasn't a man to waste time. She was now convinced of it. He hadn't even been inside before he'd started noting the pros and cons of his possible investment. If the thoughtful furrows in his brow were any indication, he was already thinking in terms of illegal entry, increased insurance rates, replacement costs and potential claims for bodily injury.

"I don't make it a habit," she assured him, because she really wasn't careless. "Are they still out there?"

"They left when they saw me."

The scowl undoubtedly did it, she thought. And his size.

He still didn't strike her as the total jock-type the way his partner had. He seemed more urbane than that. Still, there was no denying the large and commanding quality about the man. "Was the older one wearing a Mariners ball cap and the other a red knit hat and a fatigue jacket?"

"You know them?"

"I know they're not dangerous," she assured him. "They come around every day when I close for the afternoon. They just had lunch, so they were probably finishing their coffee. May I take your coat?"

His frown remained. It just changed quality as he set down his briefcase. Shrugging off his outerwear, he handed it over with a distracted "Thanks," and absently straightened the jacket of his beautifully tailored suit.

The fabric of his overcoat held the heat of his body, and the subtle scents of fresh air and something woodsy and warm. She'd breathed in that unforgettable combination before.

Now, the scents brought back the memory of what she'd spent two days trying to forget: the feel of his hand protectively circling her arm, and the stabilizing calm in his deep voice when he'd warned her of the couple she'd have undoubtedly mowed down in her haste to leave the hotel.

Realizing she was hugging his coat, hoping he hadn't noticed, she murmured, "You're welcome," and headed for her office to hang it behind the door.

"Do they come around every day?" he asked, following.

"Only when it's not raining. I think they stay at a shelter or wherever it is they sleep when the weather's bad." She didn't know what to make of the disapproval in his tone any more than she did the unconscious need she'd felt to hold in his warmth. It wasn't as if the admittedly disreputable-looking men hung around out front and scared away customers. Unless someone walked past the alley on their way up or down the block, no one would even know they were there. "I usually have a couple of servings of the previous night's specials left over, so that's what I give them. If I don't have that, I make them a sandwich and give them whatever soup I've made for the day.

"In return," she pointed out, talking from the other side of her office door, "they pick up any trash the wind has blown into the alley. Since they're out there for a while when I'm here alone this time of day, I don't have to worry if I need to leave the back door unlocked, like I did for you."

"But you don't know anything about them," he concluded from the hallway.

His tone was as flat as the crepes she'd had on the menu for breakfast. When she opened the door, his expression held that same dispassion.

"Nothing about them personally, no," she confirmed. "I'll admit they creeped me out a little at first, but they seemed grateful and respectful and in the year they've been coming around, they've given me no reason to worry." She offered a faint smile, hoping to coax one out of him. "No more than any of the customers I also don't know who come in my front door, anyway," she qualified. "I'm okay with them there."

For a moment, Max said nothing. He just kept his focus on the acceptance in her eyes, partly to keep it from straying to the smooth skin exposed by the almost careless way the top of her jacket was unbuttoned. Mostly, though, because he didn't know what to make of her defense of a couple of homeless guys most people would have run off or reported for vagrancy.

The way he often had been in his youth.

The errant thought came out of nowhere. Unexpected.

Unwanted. And just as immediately banished as completely irrelevant. His past was just that. Past. Over. Done with.

"You're not usually alone when customers are out front."

Having pointed that out, he told himself to leave it be. It was her business he needed to focus on. Nothing else. If he found her bistro an appropriate investment, he could get into her general security measures later. Scott could worry about her personal safety.

"I've gone over what you gave me," he continued, certain he had his priorities straight. "If you'll give me your payroll records, inventories and about a half an hour, we can talk. I'll need your tax returns, too."

"I have everything right here."

Looking as anxious as she sounded to get his audit over with, she turned to one of the filing cabinets beside her desk. Pulling the files he'd requested, she stacked them on the desk and turned to where he waited for her to come out. As cramped as her office was they'd pretty much be bumping elbows in there together.

Seeming aware of that herself, she turned sideways when he did to slip past him in the doorway. Even then, their bodies brushed. As they did, her back bumped the door frame.

Without thinking, he caught her by the upper arms.

Their contact was brief, the skim of clothing rather than flesh as he turned her around so she was in the hall. Still, beneath his hands, he felt her supple, feminine muscles tense. His own body had already gone tight from the faint scents of lemon and something herbal clinging to her skin. Or maybe what he caught was the scent of her hair; her shampoo, or whatever she used to make it so shiny.

It had just occurred to him that he had no idea how something so innocent could smell so erotic when he let his hands slip away. He could still recall the feel of her slender muscles when he'd curled his hand around her arm the other day; the way they'd tensed, then, almost instinctively relaxed before she'd leaned into him.

Conscious of her all over again, he took a step back.

"Sorry," he murmured.

"It's a tight space." Offering the excuse with an uncertain little smile, she took a step away herself. "We're always bumping into each other back here."

When he'd first come in, he'd thought she'd looked a little pale. At the time, it had seemed that heat from the ovens baking things that smelled incredible would have put a little color in her cheeks. But that had been before he'd glimpsed the gentle curve of her breast and he'd found himself totally sidetracked by the too-appealing lines of her body.

Her color definitely looked better now as she stood with one hand splayed below her throat. What had the bulk of his attention, though, was the way her forearm covered where his jacket had grazed hers. It was almost as if she'd felt something in that fleeting contact, too, and wasn't yet ready to let it go.

Seeming conscious of what she'd just betrayed, her hand fell. "I'm sorry. I forgot to ask. Would you like coffee? Or something to eat?"

Far more aware of her than he wanted to be, far more aware than he *should* be, he shrugged off his jacket.

"Coffee would be great."

"Regular or French press?"

"French press is more work."

"But it's better."

Telling himself her soft smile had nothing to do with his choice, he murmured, "French press, then. Black." Calling, "Thanks," as she walked away, he dropped his jacket over the back of the chair, rolled up his sleeves and pulled his calculator and the file he'd had Margie open on her from his briefcase.

Concentrating on her books was exactly the distraction he needed. What he didn't need was the vague restlessness she'd increased somehow, and that lingered even as he settled at her desk and flipped open her files.

Within minutes, though, that edgy sensation had been buried by bafflement.

He'd already had Margie run the usual preliminary credit checks on her. Beyond the fact that Ms. Fairchild's credit was excellent, he'd found there was no record of any initial loan, open or closed, for the restaurant. Likewise for any student loans. The SBA loan she'd mentioned was nearly paid off. She had credit cards, but owed nothing on them. The only car she'd financed, a small, sporty but practical now five-year-old SUV, had been paid off two years ago.

He had no idea where her initial funding had come from. He would have thought she'd saved it herself somehow. But her profit and loss statement indicated that she hadn't a clue how to save a dollar, much less the thousands it would have taken to get her business up and running.

A look at her website last night had only raised more questions. The short paragraph about the restaurant that served "the best of the Northwest in a rustic, provincial style," had also mentioned that Chef Fairchild was a graduate of a local culinary institute of some note, that she'd taken courses in Paris and Nice, and that she'd worked under chefs of considerable renown at two of the most prestigious restaurants in town.

The studies in Paris and Nice had caught his attention. Someone had had to pay for that. Even if she'd earned a scholarship, travel expense would have been involved.

His first thought had been that her family had paid for her education, thus the lack of student loans and the ability to travel abroad. Some parents did that, or so he'd heard.

He hadn't had that privilege. Or the family for that matter. As he'd been reminded minutes ago, his own roots were considerably meaner, and definitely leaner, than those of the people he associated with now. But she'd insisted that her family hadn't been involved in her career at all. Since the background check they ran as a precaution to uncover possible fronting operations hadn't come back yet, he had no idea if they would have been able to help her, anyway.

He'd gleaned nothing else from the site, other than an unusual craving for the crab cakes described on the menu of her seasonal fare. Those offerings came with the warning that they could change, sometimes daily, depending on what was freshest from the sea and the local organic markets.

He'd yet to taste her food, but if it was anywhere near as excellent as the heaven in a mug she'd silently set at his elbow, it was easy to see how she'd earned her reviews. As he perused the records in front of him, vaguely aware of the rattles and bumps coming from the kitchen, it was her business acumen he seriously questioned.

Tommi gave the colander in her hands a shake as she stood at the metal sink. Distracted by worry over what could be taking Max so long and with the water splashing over the spinach she rinsed, it took a moment for the knocking to register.

"Yoo-hoo, Tommi" came the muffled warble of a familiar female voice. Another knock sounded on her back door. "Are you in there?"

"It's just us," her male counterpart announced.

The colander landed in the sink with a clatter. Turning

off the tall, goose-necked faucet, Tommi grabbed a towel and headed across her kitchen, wiping her hands on the way. The Olsons never showed up before five o'clock. It was barely four-thirty.

Reaching the heavy back door, she pushed it open with a concerned, "Essie?" as cold air rushed in. "Is everything all right?"

"Everything's just fine." Her white-haired, eighty-something neighbor offered the smiling dismissal with a wave of her arthritic hand. "I hope you don't mind that we're early. Syd thought we should call down to make sure you were here and have you unlock the door. But I figured if you were out, we'd have just taken ourselves a little extra exercise."

Certain of her welcome, the woman who'd always reminded Tommi of a slightly eccentric Mrs. Claus walked in with her spry though equally aged husband at her elbow. Both wore running shoes and fleece jogging suits; his black with a white racing stripe, hers purple with pink.

Considering the neon-bright coral lipstick she wore, the woman was getting more color-blind by the day.

"We can't watch our shows," Syd muttered on his way past. "Didn't make sense to sit there doing nothing, so we thought we'd see what you're cooking up for supper tonight." Behind his black-rimmed trifocals, his keen eyes narrowed as they swept her kitchen. As if drawn by a beam, his attention fixed on the dessert rack in back.

Essie's focus remained on Tommi. "I just hope whatever it is, that you'll be eating some of it yourself," she admonished her, a tsk in her voice. "I know you said you weren't dieting, child, but I swear you look thinner every time I see you."

"Oh, leave her be, Essie."

"Well, she does, Syd. That top is practically hanging on her."

The top Tommi wore was hardly "hanging"—though she had actually lost five pounds in the past few months. They happened to be five of the ten she constantly battled, but she knew her changing shape would be showing soon enough. She wasn't as flat as she had been in some places and was definitely thicker in others. All that concerned her at the moment, however, was that she had no idea what else the always outspoken woman was about to observe. With Max within earshot, she just knew she didn't want to find out.

"Why can't you watch your shows?"

"I hit a wrong button on a remote control," Syd confessed, altering the reason for his wife's frown. "Now we can't get anything. We don't want to bother you with it, but maybe Andrew can take a look at it when he gets here. These things don't tend to confound you young people the way they do Essie and me. He'll be here soon, won't he?"

Andrew, her part-time waiter and a full-time starving artist, wasn't working that evening. Shelby would be there, though. She told them that, thinking as she did that she could have checked on their little problem herself in a while had Max not been there. But he was, and because she wanted to avoid the inevitable questions his presence would raise, she decided to hustle the Olsons out front and asked if they wanted to eat now or wait until her cassoulet was ready.

As she'd suspected they'd do, they opted to wait because they liked to eat with the "youngsters," as they called her employees. They did accept her offer of hot tea, though, and had just about vacated her kitchen for their usual table nearest the kitchen doors when Max walked out of her office carrying his cup.

As small as the area was, he'd had to hear their every word. From the way he abruptly came to a halt, it seemed he'd taken the last few moments of quiet to mean they were already gone.

Syd and Essie stared up at him. Almost in unison, the couple who'd been married for the better part of sixty years looked from the rolled sleeves of his white shirt to the sharp crease in his slacks and bounced bespectacled glances toward Tommi.

With his quietly powerful presence leaving them temporarily mute—and her feeling trapped—she focused on what he held. "More coffee?"

"I didn't mean to interrupt," Max said as she took his cup. Aware of her quick disquiet, wondering why that odd unease was there, he gave the couple eyeing him an acknowledging nod.

The thin, elderly man holding open one of the swinging doors possessed a truly impressive, electrified shock of gray hair. Beside him, a rounded little woman with snow-white curls and bright coral lips cradled a basket of bread.

"Essie and Syd, this is Max Callahan. Max," Tommi said before either could voice the speculation adding more creases to their respective brows, "this is Mr. and Mrs. Olson. They live upstairs."

The old gentleman stuck out his hand. "We're two doors down from Tommi."

"We didn't know you had company, dear."

The woman's comment held far more interest than apology. While Max shook hands with her husband, she blatantly checked out the cut of his hair, the breadth of his shoulders, his watch and the shine on his shoes.

Her smile went as bright as her lipstick. "You should have said something when we got here."

"Oh, he isn't... You aren't..." As quickly as Tommi sought to disabuse the woman of her notions, she just as quickly cut herself off. "Mr. Callahan is a...business associate."

"It's Max." Tommi clearly didn't want to be rude. It seemed just as apparent that she didn't care to share the nature of the business that had him coming out of her minuscule office in his shirtsleeves. "I'm just going over some numbers for her," he said, keeping everything simple.

Disappointment removed the odd and sudden hope from the older woman's expression. "Ah. You're her accountant, then." The pronouncement came with the knowing lift of her chin. "I just thought maybe our Tommi finally had herself a boyfriend. Her youngest sister just got engaged. Bobbie," she explained, just in case he didn't know. "Sweet girl. We'd love to see Tommi find a man of her own, too, but all she does is work." Her head leaned at a considering tilt. "Are you married?"

Tommi set down Max's cup with a discomfited clink. "Let's get you seated, Essie. Then I'll get your tea. And I need to get Max's coffee," she insisted, as the elderly lady opened her mouth as if to say she wasn't done yet. "Come on. I'll bring you the blend I just got from that new organic company I'm using. Mango green. You'll love it."

It seemed as clear to Max as the small diamonds winking from Tommi's earlobes that she had no intention of allowing her private life—or apparent lack thereof—to be discussed any further. At least, not in front of him. With a smile that actually looked rather sweet given the determination behind it, she walked straight past him to nudge the vociferous Essie from the kitchen.

Syd caught the door as they passed, pushing it back

far enough to lock open. Instead of following the women, though, he turned back with a thoughtful frown furrowing his weathered face.

"Can you fix a television remote control?"

Growing more confused by the moment with the owner of the little establishment, the old guy's question caught Max totally off guard. So did the fact that it had been addressed to him.

Apparently, in Tommi's bistro, there were no strangers.

"I don't know," he hedged. "That would depend on what's wrong with it."

"I can't tell you that. All I know is I went to change the channel to get Essie's soap opera and the screen went blue. She said I used the wrong remote. We have three of 'em," he muttered. "They all look the same to me."

It sounded to Max as if the guy had switched from the television to the DVD. He'd just mentioned that when Tommi came back in, touching the man's shoulder on her way past.

"Don't worry about it, Syd. I'll make sure it gets taken care of. The new *Weekly* came this morning," she told him, her voice drifting behind her as she spoke of a local free paper. "I left a couple of copies on the table.

"Here," she said, doing an about-face to hand him a pencil she'd just retrieved. "Essie needs this to do the crossword puzzle."

"Is my letter to the editor in there?"

"I haven't had a chance to look."

The problem with the remote had just been preempted. Turning with the squeak of rubber soles on tile, Syd made a beeline into the bistro. As he did, Tommi headed the opposite way, a trail of consternation following in her wake.

"I'm sorry about that," she murmured, but didn't stop

until she'd snagged two white ceramic teapots and a French press from a rack destined for the coffee and wine bar out front.

Because the door remained open, Max joined her where she worked at the prep station in the middle of the kitchen. His voice went low. "I thought you were closed until five-thirty."

"I am. The Olsons aren't customers." Her own voice remained equally hushed as she turned to fill the teapots with hot water from the Insta-Hot, then turned back to spoon coffee into the tall, clear press carafe. "They come down to critique my specials for me. They're just early today."

"They critique your food?"

Beneath the jacket he'd heard the older lady claim was hanging on her, one shoulder lifted in a small shrug.

"In a way."

He heard evasion in her response, saw a hint of it in her expression. What he saw mostly as he deliberately refrained from more closely eyeing the fit of her jacket himself was unease. "By any chance would 'in a way' mean they don't pay for their meals?"

"I can't take their money."

"Why not?"

"They're on a pension," she said, totally missing the point of his question.

Her specials ran from thirteen to twenty-seven dollars. He knew because he'd been running totals of her diligently calculated costs of each serving. She likewise kept track of meals served, as would any restaurateur worth a grain of the imported salt she ordered from the coast of France. It was the missing profit between the two he couldn't find.

Leaving his carafe after she'd set in the filter plate and plunger, she set the teapots and accessories on a tray. Instead of picking up the tray, though, she suddenly stopped, took a deep breath and met his eyes.

"Thank you, Max."

"For what?"

"For going along with Essie's assumption that you're my accountant. They're very nice people. They truly are. They just like to share everything they hear."

It was their main source of recreation, actually, she thought.

"As I said the other day," she continued, terribly conscious of how close she and Max were standing, "I need to keep the partnership business quiet for now. Syd and Essie know my family. It wouldn't be at all unusual for them to mention that you were here if one of them came in. Since my sisters know my accountant isn't a male—" much less the very attractive, distracting, and successful-looking one Essie would no doubt describe "—they'd have questions."

Her glance faltered. "I need time to explain why I'm entering into a partnership. If a partnership works out," she qualified, taking nothing for granted where he was concerned. "So the less said to anyone, the better."

Thinking she'd be a disaster at poker, Max tipped his head to see her eyes. "I'm missing something here." She wasn't comfortable. Not with him. Not with the situation. Not with whatever it was she was keeping from him and, he suspected, everyone else.

"I understand wanting to wait to mention a partnership to your staff. Employees get nervous when they hear rumors about a change in ownership status."

"Exactly. I don't want them worrying."

"Got that," he assured her, though he thought more in terms of staff bailing out over rumors of change. "What I don't get is what's so complicated about your family knowing you want the partnership so you can hire another chef."

His eyes narrowed on the quick evasion in hers. "Do they have something to do with the personal thing you mentioned the other day?"

She ducked her head, the overhead lights catching glints of gold in her dark hair as she picked up the tray with the tea.

"Look," she murmured. "It's nothing. Nothing," she repeated, and nodded toward his coffee. "That will take a few minutes to steep. I'll bring it in to you when it's ready."

With a grace that totally belied her agitation, she slipped through the open doorway, leaving him staring at her slender back. Wondering at her contradictions, impressed by the sheer number of them, his suspicion turned to absolute certainty.

If he'd learned anything about women in the past thirty-eight years, it was that *nothing* always meant *something*. And there was now no doubt in his mind that Tommi Fairchild had something on hers that she wasn't sharing.

He wanted to know what that something was. But the fact that it was personal gave him pause. No one understood the need to keep certain information private better than he did. Particularly when it involved a person's family. Not that he had any idea what family was supposed to be. The whole concept was pretty much foreign to him.

Unlike Tommi, he didn't talk about his relatives. There wasn't a thing he could say about his lineage that wouldn't earn him scorn or a cold shoulder in certain circles, or evoke pity in others. He never lied about his past. He just judiciously omitted certain details about how he'd made it through school and precisely where he'd lived growing up. As for his one attempt to create a family of his own, his short-lived marriage to Jenna Walsh had ended shortly after her old boyfriend decided he wanted her back. Its demise had also left him with her bills and a profound appreciation for the benefits of remaining unencumbered.

With the clench of his jaw, he cut off the ancient memories. What he needed to concentrate on was how he'd deal with the woman heading back to her kitchen. Tommi's approach to finances was the polar opposite of his own. He would keep his focus on that, not on her unwitting reminders of his past, and definitely not on the softness of her tentative smile when she walked in to see him waiting for her. He would even let go of his curiosity about whatever it was she insisted was "nothing."

For now.

Chapter Four

Tommi had expected Max to return to her ledgers while his coffee brewed. Finding him right where she'd left him by the plating station, not trusting the speculation sharpening his sculpted features, she quickly checked the digital timers ticking down on two of the ovens and the stock pots simmering on the stove.

"Did you want something else?" she asked, torn between the need to keep him from pressing about the little secret she guarded, and the need to get to the rollitini she'd barely started.

"Just to talk to you. I'm finished with your books."

Her breath slithered out.

"Oh," she murmured, anxiety taking another shift. "Is here okay?"

When he had first arrived, all she'd wanted was to know if her bistro interested him. As torn as she was about giving up the total control she now had over her business, her impatience seemed truly ironic.

That finer point was lost, however, as she closed the kitchen door. She felt bad doing that. The Olsons didn't come only for a meal. They came for her company, and that of her staff.

"There's more room here than in the office, and I need to keep an eye on things in the oven."

"Here works."

"Then, I'll prepare you something while we talk," she said, on her way to the refrigerator. "I'm sure you'll want to taste my food before you make any decisions."

"Your food is exceptional."

She'd made it as far as the plating station. "You've never tasted it."

"Actually, I have. I asked my assistant and some of our accounting staff to eat lunch here yesterday. I also had Margie bring me takeout."

"Margie?"

"My assistant. Even if I hadn't," he continued easily, "it's obvious your food brings people in. You're not in a location where you can count on a lot of foot traffic. We'll get to that later, though," he promised. "Right now, we need to talk about your expenses."

Leaning against the work counter across from her, he crossed his long legs at his ankles and his arms over his broad chest. With his hands tucked as they were, the crisp white fabric of his dress shirt stretched across his shoulders and pulled across honed biceps. "You have a serious problem with cost containment."

Tommi jerked her attention from all that nicely dressed, hard male muscle. She was still back at the part where he'd had his secretary take him takeout. She wanted to know what he'd ordered. The only to-go she could remember offhand was for a panini and crab cakes. "I do?"

"You do," he assured her. "Let's start with your employees.

Your records show that you only have four regulars on the payroll. I have no idea how you're running this place with such low staffing—"

"Oh, we do fine," she said before he could add the "but" to his sentence. She spoke quickly, apparently not wanting him to think her physical management of her business as deficient as her financial skills.

"Alaina covers breakfast and lunch and Shelby does lunch and dinner. Shelby teaches a spin class at the gym while we're closed in the afternoon," she explained, accounting for the longer hours. "Andrew works dinner with Shelby Thursday through Saturday. Since those are our busy nights, that's when Mario comes in to bus tables, do dishes and help me mop up."

Which apparently left her with the cleanup the rest of the week, he realized. "And if one of them can't make it?"

"I call Bobbie. My sister."

"Isn't she the one who just got engaged?"

His question gave Tommi pause.

"Just last week, actually." And now that Bobbie would be getting married, Tommi knew she wouldn't have anywhere near the extra time she'd once had. Or the need for the money. Aside from having finally found her calling as head of Golden Ability Canine Assistance and being the almost-new-stepmom of two, Bobbie's fiancé seemed intent on spoiling her silly. All of which was wonderful for her little sister—but only added another disconcerting change to the others happening in her own life.

"Bobbie always helped out in a pinch." In an emergency, she probably still would. If she could. But Tommi wouldn't impose on her time with her new family.

It was time to consider other options.

"Frankie has helped out once in a while, too," she continued, though she immediately ruled her out as a possible permanent fill-in. Brainy and highly educated, her second oldest sister seemed to enjoy the diversion of serving the bistro's patrons. Especially the sometimes smart-ass but harmless guys who occasionally hung out at the wine bar. But Frankie was a university research assistant with a full life of her own.

"You have two sisters?"

"Three. Georgie is the oldest. She's far too busy to help, though." Not that Tommi would ever ask. Her hugely successful, accomplished and very sophisticated first-born sibling had far more important things to do than help out in a bistro that, at capacity, only seated twenty-eight, wine bar included. Georgie was into causes on a much larger scale. "She works for a philanthropy and travels a lot."

"Interesting names," Max muttered.

She gave a little shrug, reached for a pair of gray oven mitts. Growing up, her feeble attempt to set herself apart from "the Fairchild girls" had been to spell her name without the ending "e" like her sisters. Her rebellions had always been subtle. "We were supposed to have been George, Jr., Frank, Thomas and Robert. Our dad wanted boys."

He'd noticed on her driver's license that her name was Thomasina Grace. At the time, the name had struck him as rather formal, almost regal, in a way. Now, watching her pull on the bulky mitts and open the nearest oven's door, he couldn't help but think it a lot of name for such an unassuming woman.

Tommi fit her. Though she possessed a certain, almost casual refinement, the tomboy quality of her nickname better suited the subtle restlessness that always seemed to keep her moving.

He knew exactly how the need to keep moving felt. That restive, unsettled mental energy had driven him for years.

Not caring to consider why his own restiveness was there, more interested in what pushed her, he jerked his focus to the large and heavy-looking pan on the rack she'd pulled out. Whatever it was had a mahogany crust and smelled incredible.

"So which is it?" he asked, as she pressed the crust down and ladled thick, rich broth over the top. "You do or you don't have some sort of emergency staffing in place?"

"Not emergency," she admitted. "When I need extra help serving or prepping for a private party, I make arrangements ahead of time with the culinary school. The students get credit for real-world experience," she explained with a smile. "But I'll get something figured out. Soon."

He had the feeling she was helping those students out as much as they were her. What he liked was that the help was free.

"Then, that brings me back to the rest of what I was going to say. I'm not sure how you run this place with such low regular staffing," he repeated, his attention divided between the appealing curve of her mouth and what looked like some sort of casserole, "but you obviously manage. My concern is that you only have four employees, but your total payroll dollars equal wages and benefits for twice that many."

"Twice? My math isn't that far off, is it? I always double-check it."

"It's not your math. It's what you're paying. You show a base pay for each employee that's nearly double what other restaurants offer.

"Then, there's insurance," he continued, before she could ask what was wrong with that. "I don't know a company in this industry who pays for so much coverage for their employees. Those two things right there are a big part of why your profits are almost half of what they should be."

He wasn't at all surprised that she'd been turned down for a loan. Had he been a banker, he would have done the same. Looking at the business as a potential investment, though, even a minor one, he could see where there were significant profits to be made. With some equally significant changes. "Cut those expenses and you'll save thousands a year."

Tommi felt her back go up. She wasn't about to cut her employees' pay. Or their benefits. Needing to hear him out, though, she calmly asked, "Enough to hire another chef?"

"Not enough for that. But there are other things that can be done to pay for him, pay for more waitstaff and turn a better profit." He eyed her evenly. "You could even take a real salary for yourself."

Tommi kept ladling. He'd obviously figured out that pretty much everything she made went back into the business. What he didn't seem to understand was that, except for backup, she didn't need more waitstaff.

She could seriously get into the more profit part, though. More profit meant she would be able to pay for the babysitter she would eventually need. And for a larger apartment. The Williamses down the hall from her were moving in a few months and their two bedroom would be available. It even had a view of the little park across the street.

Thinking of the park reminded her that she'd need to buy a buggy, then a stroller. And a bassinet, a crib, a car seat.

"How much of a salary?"

"At a minimum, double what you're drawing now." From the corner of her eye, she saw him motion toward the pan. "What is that?"

She'd just considered that double would be good and was about to add "rocking chair" to her mental list when she became conscious of the nerves jumping in her stomach. The disturbing direction of their conversation was only partly responsible for the sensation. Some of it came with the alternating panic and wonder that came whenever she thought of her impending motherhood.

The rest had to do with Max, and the way he watched her every move. Specifically with the way he watched her mouth when she spoke and the feel of his glance moving down her throat.

Already far more aware of him than she wanted to be, she reached under the plating station and pulled out a shallow bowl. "Cassoulet," she replied, now conscious of his eyes on the nape of her neck. "It's a peasant dish from the south of France."

"What's in it?"

"In this one, there's chicken, pork, bacon, sausage, seasonings and white beans." Ladling a scoop into the center of the bowl, far more comfortable with her food than his effect on her nervous system, she told him that the French usually used duck confit with garlic sausages and bacon. "Basically it's a stew of white beans and meats." Closing the oven, she added a fork to the bowl and handed the bowl to him. "The best part is the crust.

"So aside from cutting wages and benefits," she continued, leaving him to contemplate what she'd just given him, "what are the other things I can do to make a better profit?"

Glancing back, she saw him poke at a bite of beans and sausage.

"You could relocate."

She went utterly still.

He didn't seem to notice. His attention remained on the meat he lifted with his fork, then let cool a moment before he tasted it. After a quick pause, his eyebrows rose in silent approval.

"Relocate?" she asked, too busy rejecting the possibility to care about his obvious approval of her current house specialty.

He forked up another bite.

"Just hear me out." He sounded as if he'd expected resistance. He just didn't seem too concerned about it as he settled more comfortably against the counter. "You didn't add to the few dollars you spent on advertising when you started staying open for dinner, but your dinner business picked up pretty quickly. You only have an ad in one free local magazine, a website and phone listing. What do you think brings in your customers?"

The man had obviously known what he was looking for in her books. Since he hadn't answered her question, though, she wasn't totally sure where he was going with his.

"Mostly word of mouth. And the reviews."

"What keeps them coming back?"

"The service. The food. The atmosphere."

The nod he gave was thoughtful. She just couldn't tell if he was considering what she'd said, or what he was eating.

With the timer about to go off on the other oven, she grabbed her mitts again, pulled out the baguette slices she'd left crisping and slid them onto a cooling rack.

"Exactly my point," he informed her, eyeing what she would serve under melted Gruyère in French onion soup with the same curiosity he had the fullness of her lower lip. "People come here because they like what you've created, not because you're convenient. That was mentioned in your reviews," he reminded her. "You're not near anywhere most people are likely to be going. All you have here is a neighborhood of old apartment buildings that are stalled on their renovation.

"On this block you have a dry cleaner and a bookstore. The storefront next door is empty. When I was in the other day, most of your customers didn't appear to be tenants of these buildings. Since they were leaving in cabs, I assume they came from uptown. If you're doing as well as you are here, imagine what you'd do in a better location.

"That was great, by the way," he said, holding out the suddenly empty bowl.

She should have felt pleased by his unqualified assessment. She supposed that at some level she was. It was just that the pleasure she usually took in knowing her efforts were appreciated happened to be buried under a pile of disagreement and misgivings.

"Thanks," she murmured, and set the bowl in the sink.

The large pan of bread pudding sat cooling near the chocolate tortes she'd prepared that morning. Since it now had his attention, she disappeared into the refrigerator and walked back out with a stainless-steel bowl full of the crème fraîche she'd made yesterday.

On her way to the pudding, she picked up a dessert plate.

Resistance was veiled by an accommodating, deceptive calm. "Where would you suggest I move to?"

He recommended one of the more affluent, upscale walking neighborhoods. Magnolia, Queen Anne, Capitol Hill. "This area has the potential of being a draw when all the renovation is finished around here," he then admitted, "but that's probably another five to ten years off. You have a good concept. It could be great in a better location."

She couldn't argue with his assessment of the little neighborhood. The area was so nondescript it didn't even rate a name. It was simply a quiet, tree-lined spot in the city that hadn't made it through the transition it had struggled for years to make. But it was affordable, the people were friendly and despite the skeletal scaffolding on the empty buildings on some of the blocks, the place was charming in its own modest way.

As for her concept, he didn't understand it at all.

"Cut my employees' pay and relocate." Having recapped what he'd said would be necessary so far, she dished pudding onto the plate and topped it with the crème and a dusting of nutmeg. She had no intention of doing either, but he'd come all this way. She should at least feed him while she heard him out just in case he came up with something she could actually use.

"What else?" she asked, and held out the plate.

Max didn't trust her almost studied calm as he took what she offered. He'd have thought for certain that she would balk at his conclusions. He just didn't get a chance to wonder what he was missing as he searched her face, or to respond to what she'd asked.

Syd walked in carrying a magazine-like newspaper. Pointing to the page he held up, the elderly gentleman grinned at Tommi.

"They printed my letter," he announced. "They edited it by half, but the gist is still there.

"See?" he said, including Max as he angled the page toward him.

Tommi's smile came quickly. So did her congratulations. But Syd's train of thought had just totally derailed. He'd no sooner lowered the paper than he noticed the plate in Max's hand.

"That'll take you home, son. It sure does me. She makes good cobblers, but you can't beat her bread pudding. I think it's the extra butter and cinnamon."

Swallowing a mouthful of it, Max's only response was an unexpected, and agreeing, nod. The old guy was right. It did take him back. But not to his own home. What the bready custard instantly reminded him of was sitting at the rickety table in an old next-door neighbor's kitchen. The lady, Mrs. Hopp, he remembered, had watched him in the evening while his mom worked her second job.

He remembered little else about the woman, other than that she'd seemed huge, that she'd been nice to him, and that after she'd moved, he'd had to stay by himself at night.

He couldn't have been more than eight or nine at the time.

The memory wasn't particularly bad. Not like so many others he'd buried. It just…was.

The plate clinked softly against the work surface as he set it down.

When he looked up, it was to see Tommi's quick concern.

"Is something wrong with it?"

That old memory had just brought another—of him lying to his mother about sleeping in the closet because he'd been playing fort rather than admit he'd been afraid and risk seeing her cry.

Ruthlessly cutting off the thought, deliberately avoiding Tommi's eyes, he forced a smile.

"Not at all. Syd's right. It does take you home.

"So, what's your letter about?" he asked Syd, thinking any subject preferable to the past he'd been utterly determined to escape.

The old guy pushed up the bridge of his dark-rimmed trifocals.

"It's about all the condo conversions going on around here. These developers come in, buy up the old apartment buildings and kick out the tenants to do their renovating," he muttered. "Then the folks can't move back because they can't afford to buy a unit, or to pay more rent to whoever did buy it, so they have to start all over away from their old neighbors..."

Two double raps on the back door underscored Syd's lament. Wondering vaguely if Layman & Callahan invested in what concerned her, too, when she had the energy to worry about it, Tommi glanced at the security monitor—and stifled a groan on her way to let Shelby in.

She hadn't realized how late it was getting. She opened in half an hour and she still had major prep work to do.

"Thanks, Tommi," her waitress murmured, closing out the cold.

Unzipping her shiny silver raincoat, Shelby automatically started for the office to stow her purse, wraps and gym bag. Three steps later, her smile went from bright for the man whose electrified hair could give Einstein a run for his money, to curiosity for the imposing businessman towering beside him.

"Hey," she said, recognition in her kohl-rimmed eyes. "You were in here the other day."

"He's Max. Tommi's accountant," Syd told her. Still totally focused on his cause, he held out his magazine. "They published it."

"Your letter? That's awesome, Syd!"

"Is that you, Shelby?"

"It's me, Essie," she called back, wrestling off her coat. "I'll be right there. I need to get rid of my stuff."

Tommi stepped forward, holding out her hands. "Give me your things. I need to talk to Max in my office, so I'll put them away. Do me a favor and get their salads, will you?"

With an easy "Sure thing," her spike-haired server handed over coat and bags.

"Come on, Syd," Shelby continued, edging the man she regarded as a surrogate grandfather toward the door. "I want to read your letter. Did they leave in the part about 'indigenous economic inequity'?"

"Nah," he muttered as they headed out. "They cut that part."

"She eats here, too?" Max asked as they disappeared.

"All my staff does."

"What sort of a discount do you give them on their meals?"

Except for the vague unrest she'd sensed before about him, nothing betrayed the quick distance she'd noticed when he'd set aside the dessert she'd given him, and which she'd immediately taken away. She'd hoped he'd enjoy what she'd offered. Instead, it had clearly reminded him of something he didn't care to dwell on. Just as clear from his comment was that whatever that something was had to do with his childhood.

The realization had brought a quick stab of sympathy. She knew how hard some childhood memories could be. Yet, what she felt as she motioned him toward her office was the need to defend herself.

"I don't give them a discount. Their meals are free because they need to eat and I want them to know what we're serving our guests. I'm sure you know that it's easier to answer questions about a dish if you've actually tasted it."

In the space of seconds, she'd hung Shelby's coat on the peg beside Max's, stowed everything else in the bottom filing cabinet drawer where her staff kept their things and turned to the man filling her doorway.

Max studied her openly, doing nothing at all to mask that unapologetic scrutiny. The way his eyes narrowed on her face made her feel as if she were some sort of specimen on a slide, something vaguely incomprehensible to him. Or, maybe, something…hopeless.

"Come in, will you?" she asked, moving as far back as she could from whatever conclusions he was drawing. And to make room for him. Shelby would be returning to the kitchen. There was only one way to insure that they wouldn't be overheard. "And close the door?"

Between the computer desk, filing cabinets and book-cases, the eight-by-ten foot rectangle of space was tight to begin with. The quiet click of the door latch seemed to reduce its size by half.

Being trapped in such close confines with all that latent tension was simply one more reason to get what she had to say over with.

"I truly appreciate you coming here. I really do," she admitted, sincerely. "But I'm afraid we're not on the same page at all. You're talking about me needing to do things that I just can't do."

One dark eyebrow arched. "Can't?"

"Won't," she quietly amended. "I won't cut my employees' pay. Except for Mario, they've all been with me since the day I opened. Mario's been here for nearly that long." For all she knew, the man silently messing with her nerves had already figured that out. He had a way of gleaning information from her records that she hadn't realized was even there.

"The only night he's missed was the night of his high school graduation last June," she continued. "He just started a culinary arts course at the community college a couple of months ago and this is his only source of income.

"Alaina is a single mom." Her growing appreciation of the woman's responsibilities added a touch more defense to her tone. "She can't afford a pay cut. With three kids, she definitely can't afford to be without good insurance.

"Shelby works two jobs to support herself and her younger brother," she hurried on. "She teaches over at the gym between lunch and dinner shifts, but she does that to pay for her brother's membership. If he's there working out, she doesn't have to worry about him getting into trouble. She's also worth every dime I pay her. So is Andrew. He knows wines and remembers customers and he's a huge help when it comes to pairings. He's also a fabulous artist. He just doesn't make enough off his paintings to live on, so he really needs what he earns here.

"As for relocating," she told him, dishearteningly certain she was kissing any hope of a partnership goodbye, "if I moved across town, Syd and Essie wouldn't get a hot meal as often as they do. Essie has been afraid to cook since a pan caught fire on her stove last year and she got burned trying to put it out. Syd doesn't cook at all. Then, there's Mario. He walks here to save bus money. He couldn't do that if I move."

He regarded her with unnerving calm. "Anything else?" he asked.

She opened her mouth, closed it again. Having said what she needed to say, figuring she'd said enough, her response was the shake of her head and a quiet, "That's it."

Max couldn't remember the last time he'd witnessed that much fervor from someone who wasn't seeking something solely for herself. She had to know that refusing to cut such a huge expense could jeopardize her dealings with him. He just didn't know what to make of the odd mix of stubborn refusal and worry he sensed in her as she stood with her arms crossed, waiting for his response.

Her refusal to make changes didn't surprise him, even if her reasons did. Given how proprietary she'd sounded the other day when she'd insisted the bistro was all hers, he'd expected resistance. Like the plea that had underscored her defense, it was the worry he sensed in her that threw him.

That quiet plea lingered in her eyes, too genuine to succumb to her attempt to blink it away, too desperate to exist solely because she needed another chef in her kitchen.

"I didn't say you had to move for us to do business," he reminded her mildly. "I just said it would increase your profits."

She hesitated, wary as much of what he'd just said as the way the quiet tones of his voice seemed to caress her nerves. "But I'd still have to cut pay?"

"And some of the insurance."

"Both?"

"The points are non-negotiable," he explained, struck as much by her loyalty to her employees as her lack of common sense.

"What you want isn't logical," he pointed out, wondering at how that indefinable concern robbed the light from her eyes. "You don't want to cut expenses, yet you want to hire a chef that you'll pay more than you take for a salary yourself. This place isn't big enough to support two chefs at that level—that money has to come from somewhere.

"But we still have things to talk about," he assured her, wishing that light would return. He knew it existed. He'd seen it in her smile. "There are other ways to boost your bottom line. You just need to start thinking outside the box."

He didn't want her shutting the door on their company. For Scott's sake, he hurried to remind himself. And because she did have a great prototype here. He never thought small. He was sure his partner would see the franchise possibilities, too.

Concentrating on his partner's interest in this woman

seemed infinitely wiser just then than thinking about the woman herself. He couldn't believe how fragile she looked with her arms crossed so protectively. Or maybe it was the deep, shuddery breath she drew and the relieved fall of her slender shoulders that made him aware of how vulnerable she seemed.

The disquiet shadowing her eyes was what he noticed most.

That distress felt like a tangible thing to him. Drawn by it, by her, he found himself fighting the wholly unfamiliar need to touch the silky-looking skin of her cheek, and tell her she didn't need to look so concerned.

He curled his fingers into his palm as he checked the thought. He had no idea where the disturbing impulse had come from. As he turned to pull his jacket from the back of the desk chair, what he did know was that he knew little about offering reassurance to a woman—and that he had no business thinking about touching her at all.

"I'm going to run some numbers tonight and drop something off for you to look over." Mindful of the room's confines, he pushed his arms into his jacket's sleeves, shrugged it onto his shoulders. "What time do you open in the morning?"

Tommi's pulse scrambled as he turned back to her. He was closer than he'd been moments ago, close enough for her to feel the tension radiating from his big body. Close enough for that tension to taunt the nerves he'd managed to calm when he'd made it clear she hadn't killed her prospects with his company.

"Seven. But I'm usually in the kitchen by five-thirty."

His eyes held hers, unreadable despite his faint smile. "I'll be here at seven then."

She gave him a small nod, then watched his smile fade as his glance skimmed her face, and settled on her mouth.

Something shifted in his expression, something that tightened the carved angles of his face and darkened the depths of his too blue eyes. Yet, even as she felt her heart nudge her breastbone, his glance returned to hers. It was only then that she realized she was barely breathing—and that she hadn't moved.

"I need my coat," he said.

He was waiting for her to hand him his overcoat from the row of pegs beside her. Totally unnerved by his effect on her, busy masking it, she plucked the garment from its hook, held it out to him.

With a distracted "Thanks," he opened the door.

She could hear voices beyond the kitchen. Mostly, she was conscious of the man who grabbed his briefcase just before he answered the no-nonsense ring of his cell phone and walked out her back door telling his caller that he'd pay whatever was necessary to get some option back.

Needing distraction, Tommi was still wondering if she'd actually seen the heat she'd felt in Max's expression, or if her wildly fluctuating hormones had only made her imagine it, when he called at six-thirty the next morning. He wanted to know if he could stop by the bistro on his way back from the gym. He'd had a dinner last night that had led to an 8:00 a.m. meeting and he was booked solid through that evening. Dropping off what he had for her would be most convenient for him now. He could be there in five minutes.

Because she was avoiding the kitchen for the moment, specifically the cooking aromas, she'd answered the telephone under the bar in the front of the bistro. Telling him now would be fine, and to come to the front door, she hung up and finished the handful of Puff Pops slowly settling her stomach. Remembering what she'd promised a customer, feeling brave, she'd added garlic to the stock for a pot of rustic mushroom soup.

She should have held off on the bulbous herb for another week.

The raw scent was gone now, scrubbed from her hands with lemon and soap, and the bulbs were mellowing in the simmering stock. She felt infinitely better than she had a while ago. To be on the safe side, though, she wouldn't go back into the kitchen until after Max had gone.

It probably would have been safer, too, to distract herself from the memory of his unnerving effect on her yesterday. Something about him seemed to affect her on some elemental level. But she didn't have time for distractions or to figure out what that something was. He was due there any minute.

Chapter Five

Max thrived on challenge—lived for it, craved it. It didn't matter if the challenge was to shave seemingly impossible seconds from his fastest run, or close a deal others swore would collapse. It didn't always look like it to anyone else, especially those he left in his wake, but he wasn't trying to beat the next guy. He was trying to beat himself. The more successful he was, the more successful he needed to be. The need had become so ingrained he no longer knew why it was there.

He was well aware, however, that defying the odds was what drove him. As he pulled his black Mercedes coupe to the curb outside the darkened Corner Bistro, he wondered now what the odds were that the unrealistic and impractically soft-hearted Ms. Fairchild would listen to reason. Considering her reactions to his recommendations yesterday, he figured, "not good."

Considering his reactions to her, he intended to let what

he was dropping off speak for itself and be in and out of her bistro in under five minutes. He'd never regarded himself as being particularly noble, but his sense of honor wouldn't allow him to trespass on another guy's turf—even if the guy hadn't done anything but stake his claim and leave town.

That also meant he'd leave her personal life alone. Whatever it was she was keeping from everyone, Scott could handle on his own.

The streetlamps still glowed in the predawn darkness as he jogged up to the bistro's front door and rapped on the glass. Standing beneath the arched awning, he saw a slender finger lift back an edge of the long shade marked Closed. The shade had no sooner fallen back into place than he heard the metallic clicks of a latch being unbolted and a lock opening.

The moment he stepped into the warmth of the dim room, Tommi closed the door behind him. The faint scents of cinnamon and something savory drifted from the kitchen. What he noticed more was that the top buttons of the longer white chef's jacket she wore were again undone.

"This will only take a minute." Ignoring the enticing vee of skin below the hollow of her throat, he watched her slide lock and latch back into place and pulled a manila envelope from inside his sweat jacket. "I just want to point out a couple of areas on the recaps that might be confusing."

The room held little more than shades of gray. Though bright light spilled through the open kitchen door, it barely reached a dozen feet into the quiet and empty space. The only other illumination came from the cone-shaped red pendant lights and the two spotlights above the small coffee and wine bar.

The bar was where she motioned. "Let's go back there. It'll be easier to see."

With a small smile, she turned to lead him between the neatly set tables. He'd barely glimpsed her face, but the weak light made her skin look like alabaster, impossibly smooth, translucent, pale.

Despite the better light, her skin still had that pale quality when they reached the bar with its row of low stools.

Not wanting to think about her skin, the shine of her upswept hair or anything else that might distract him from his purpose, he laid the papers he'd pulled from the envelope on the bar's black-granite surface.

"These are profit projections based on two different expansion phases. The second is a continuation of the first, so it shows you how you can grow in stages."

She stood at his elbow, her attention on the sheets. He caught the soft scents of lemon and herbal shampoo. Moving the first sheet in front of her, more conscious of her scent than he wanted to be, he pointed to the bottom line.

"This is the projected difference in your gross income after a year with the first phase. I called the leasing agent for this building to get figures for leasing the vacant space next door. The initial costs of expansion would eat up a lot of the first-year profits, but after that, you'd see a forty percent increase."

He pulled the other sheet forward. "The second phase has to do with staying open seven days a week and adding catering. That will require additional staffing," he warned her, "but you'd have six months or so to work new people in."

With the bistro not yet open, the space surrounding them felt different to him. There was no clinking of utensils and glass. No murmur of conversation. No bustle. Just a tune from a radio in the kitchen that was so faint he couldn't even tell what it was. All that quiet made him even more aware of Tommi's silence as he watched her push back a strand of hair that had slipped from its clip. Her chef's cap lay on the stool beside her, set there, apparently, when she'd pulled it from her head and dislodged the strand that promptly fell back to her cheek.

She gave an almost imperceptible shake of her head.

Discouraged, trying hard not to be, Tommi looked from the neat columns of figures on the pages. His bottom lines were truly impressive. Far beyond anything she'd ever imagined possible. But then, she'd never thought in terms of large profits, or a larger place. "Bigger" had never been part of her dream. She wanted her bistro just the way it was. Small. Intimate. Hers. And hers alone.

She already knew the status quo was no longer possible. It was just hard letting go, even though she knew, too, that she would have to concede parts of her dream to keep even a modified version of that dream alive. But all she could think about just then was of how much more work his more extensive plans would involve.

He hadn't mentioned expanding yesterday. Apparently, this was his alternative to moving.

Without looking from the pages, she quietly asked, "How soon would I need to do this?"

"If we enter into an agreement within the next couple of weeks, I'd push for mid-January. Realistically, renovations would take a month. You don't want to be closed that whole time, so we could have the wall torn out in a couple of days and a temporary one erected. You could stay open here while the bulk of the work is being done on the other side."

She shook her head again, shoved her fingers through her hair. He had absolutely no idea how hard she was pushing herself already. She hadn't even made it into bed last night. When she'd finally gone upstairs, she'd lain down on her comforter, folded half of it over herself and the next thing she'd known it was five o'clock in the morning. Because she hadn't set her alarm, she'd overslept by half an hour.

"How would I pay for it?"

"We'd advance the funds as our part of the buy-in. It's all written out in the proposal in there."

Max nodded toward the envelope. After encountering her resistance yesterday, he now knew that she tended to get quiet when she was digging in her heels. Considering her now, he had the feeling she was either balking big-time or struggling hard to accept what should have been a no-brainer.

She hadn't bothered to brush the strand of hair back again.

Blocking the urge to do it himself, he pushed his hands into his pockets.

"Just look this over when you have a chance. While you're doing that," he suggested, certain she was feeling proprietary, "keep in mind that this is a business decision. Not an emotional one. It's only logical that as successful as you've been so far, you'll be an even bigger success with careful expansion."

He didn't believe emotion had any place in business. There was no room for sentiment. No logic in going with feelings. It seemed to Tommi that he couldn't have made that message any clearer had he written it across the top of each of the pages stacked so neatly in front of her.

She figured his convictions probably explained a lot about him. She just didn't attempt to figure out what all that was as she tried to imagine where she'd find the time or the energy to essentially double the bistro in size while she'd be doubling in size herself.

"I've never even considered expanding before. But I will," she assured him, wishing they could have had this conversation later in the day, when she felt more like herself.

"As for emotion, it may not have a place in business for you, but it does for me." It didn't matter that her energy was in the bucket at the moment, she needed to defend herself even if she didn't feel like it. He'd made himself clear. It only seemed fair that he know where she was coming from, too.

"This is my life," she admitted, lifting her hand in an arc to encompass the space, "so this is everything I am that we're talking about. This is *who* I am," she quietly emphasized. She looked from the kitchen doorway to the muted colors of the paintings on the walls, then to the dark windows behind her. "I can't divorce myself from what I do all that easily."

"You're going to have to learn how."

She'd followed the quick motion of her hand with her head, looked back to him just as abruptly. But feeling less than fabulous at the moment, feeling the sudden need to sit, she wasn't about to repeat her unintended performance yesterday and go toe-to-clog with his three-piece-suit, investor-knows-best insistence.

He wasn't wearing a suit right now, anyway.

And the logo on his sweat jacket seemed to be wavering.

She felt warm. She suddenly felt awfully dizzy, too. But just as she realized she'd turned her head too fast and the room started to spin, mostly what she felt was the tilt of floor.

Max saw what little color Tommi had drain from her face. Now looking as pale as milk, she lifted her hand to her head.

He was two steps away when she swayed sideways. One, when his heart jerked and her legs buckled. Catching her as she crumpled, he felt her lithe body sag against his. Chest to breast. Hard stomach to feminine belly. Thigh to thigh.

He swore. She felt as limp and light as a rag doll as he braced her behind her knees and lifted her in his arms. But even as he looked around for some place to put her, not sure at all what he'd do when he got her there, he could feel tension returning to her muscles.

She raised her head, lifting her hand as if she thought she might still be heading for the floor.

"Easy." He murmured the word, adjusting his arm across her back so her head could rest on his shoulder. "I won't let you fall."

Her response was a moan, followed by a small, "What happened?"

"You fainted. I've got you," he assured her. "Just hang on a minute."

"I'm all right."

"Like hell you are."

"I am," she insisted, her voice half a shade stronger.

"Indulge me, then. I'm going to sit you down."

Catching the lower rung of a bar stool with the toe of his running shoe, he pulled the stool out and eased her onto it. He didn't let her go, though. Her limbs still seemed weak, her movements a little slow as she touched her unsteady fingers to her forehead. Afraid she might fall over, he kept one arm across her back so her shoulder rested against his abs.

"Is anyone else here?" he asked.

She lifted her head as she gave it a shake. Apparently deciding that sort of movement wasn't a good idea, she went still and murmured, "No."

"Who do you want me to call?"

"No one. I'm okay," she repeated, her hand trembling as she pushed her hair from her face. "Really. I just need to sit here for a minute."

He could feel her warmth seeping into him. Trying to ignore the awareness of her that came with it, he eased his hand to her shoulder. With his free hand, he tipped her chin so he could see her face.

He'd wondered before if her skin would feel as soft as it looked. Skimming her cheek with his fingertips to tuck back a strand of hair she'd missed, he knew now that it felt even softer than he'd imagined.

Confusion settled in her dark eyes an instant before her lashes swept down. He barely had a chance to notice that her color seemed marginally better before she swallowed, hard, and turned her head away.

Realizing what he'd so unconsciously done, he started to pull back. No doubt his touch had just made her more uncomfortable than she already had to be.

Aware that she wouldn't look at him, he eased back far enough to be sure she would stay upright. He didn't want the concern he felt, or the uncertainty. But there were only a couple of things he could think of that might account for what had happened just now. Both could also explain why she was so desperate for help with her business.

He wanted to believe it was only practicality pushing him as he sat down close enough to catch her should the need arise.

"Are you sick, Tommi?"

There was no mistaking the guard in his tone. Certain it was there because she'd alarmed him, burning with embarrassment because of that, Tommi looked to where he sat a foot from her shoulder.

"No. No, I'm not sick. I'm perfectly healthy." Her doctor

had said so, last week, just before she'd handed her a bottle of prenatal vitamins. "Really."

Her dizziness had faded, but she still felt off balance as his questioning glance narrowed on her face. The feel of his strong arms around her, holding her, supporting her, had pulled hard at the longing deep inside her chest. She'd never felt that sort of longing before she'd met him. She hadn't even known such a feeling existed. The assurances he murmured had fed that yearning. For those brief moments, he'd let her know that she didn't need to worry, that he had her and everything else under control.

Then, there was the way he'd touched her, the unexpected and unbelievable gentleness she'd felt in him when he'd tucked back her hair.

Needing to lean on something, trying to ignore how badly she wished she could lean on him, she turned to face the bar.

With her elbows propped on it, she rested her head in her hands.

Beside her, Max angled toward the bar, too.

"Perfectly healthy," he repeated, watching her. "So if you're healthy, what caused you to turn the color of chalk and pass out?"

"I turned too fast."

"I've seen you turn faster than that," he reminded her, apparently alluding to the way she sometimes moved about her kitchen. "Has this happened before?"

"Only once. The dizziness, I mean. I was unclogging a sink the other morning. When I came out from under it, I got up too fast." She'd had to grab the sink edge to keep upright. She hadn't fainted, though. And, like now, she'd been alone. "I've never had the floor tilt like that."

"Do you know what caused it?"

Tommi dropped her hand, drew a deep breath. If she

said she didn't, she'd be lying. She could evade and avoid, but she couldn't lie. Any denial would soon come back to bite her, anyway. She wouldn't be able to hide an expanding belly forever.

What caused the dizziness had to do with things like increased blood volume and not eating properly. But she didn't bother with the literal response. Since the undeniably pragmatic man beside her tended to get straight to the point, so would she.

"I'm pregnant. Three and a half months," she said quietly. The questions would come. She might as well answer them now. "I'm due in May."

There wasn't much that truly threw Max anymore. Not about most people, and certainly not about himself. Yet, what caught him off guard just then was his gut-level reaction to what shouldn't have registered on that level at all.

The feel of her body had burned itself into his brain. Some shred of nobility, along with a hefty dose of self-preservation, hadn't allowed him to think too much about it, though. At least not until now.

As his glance moved over her, he could too easily recall the feel of her curvy little shape. The fullness of her firm breasts had pressed his chest when he'd caught her against him. When his hand had slipped along her side as he'd lifted her and when he'd helped her sit down, he'd been intensely aware of the gentle, feminine curve of her hip.

Until possibilities for her fainting had occurred to him, he never would have suspected from her slenderness that she was carrying a child. From what he'd heard from her neighbors, she didn't even have a boyfriend.

It seemed her neighbors didn't know her as well as they thought they did.

It was entirely possible that neither did his partner.

The thought brought him up short.

"Does Scott know?"

Tommi's brow furrowed. She had no idea why Max would think she'd have confided her situation to a man she'd spoken with only once since he'd stood her up. At least she didn't until she considered that his partner—and he, himself—might have concerns about her handling the workload.

"No one does. Except you. But I promise you, I can keep up. Everything I've read makes me believe I'm almost through the worst part of the morning sickness. And my energy is supposed to be coming back soon, so starting an expansion in January should be okay…if it's necessary."

All Max really knew about pregnancy was how to prevent it. His knowledge of the mysteries of a woman's body was limited strictly to how to bring pleasure. But there was no denying her conviction about the apparently diminishing physical side effects of whatever all was going on inside her. That certainty was as obvious as her hesitation about the expansion, and the silent plea in her eyes. He appreciated the conviction. It was the barely masked panic beneath the plea that he didn't want to deal with.

Her worry was showing.

Not wanting to be affected by it, he focused on the other party to her…condition. "What about the father?"

"What about him?"

"Why isn't he helping you?"

Her glance fell to a silvery vein of quartz in the granite. "Because he's gone. He went back to France right after he quit."

"Right after he quit? This is the guy who worked for next to nothing?"

"That would be him," she murmured, tracing the vein with the tip of her finger. "He was in the States to gain international experience. I did the same thing in Nice and

Paris," she said, explaining why she hadn't hesitated to hire him after a trial run in her kitchen. "Working for little more than room and board in a foreign country is a rite of passage that can earn major points on a résumé.

"Before he could get the position he wanted in Lyon, he needed a year abroad," she continued, making a short story even shorter. "But he found another position in Marseille after he started working for me." She hadn't realized at the time that he'd been looking for anything else. The entire time he'd subtly pursued her, trying to charm her, telling her maybe he should stay, he'd been looking to leave.

She hadn't believed for a moment that she was his *seul vrai amour*—his only true love. He'd said the same thing with that same charming smile and lovely accent to Alaina, Shelby, Essie and the woman who picked up and delivered the bistro's linens. He was the sort of man women adored because he was fun, exotic and made them feel good, but any woman with a soupçon of sense knew better than to take him seriously.

She'd always considered herself sensible. And practical and savvy and skeptical and all the other things a woman needed to be to make smart decisions about her life and those she allowed into it. But add a shared high for a fabulously successful private dinner for twenty and a great bottle of wine to all that European charm and her common sense had gone the way of the dodo.

Her hushed voice grew quieter. "It was one night. One night," she repeated, recrimination heavy as she slowly shook her head. "What happened should never have happened at all."

A faint edge slipped into Max's voice. "You should still get child support from him."

Never mind that she was busy beating herself up for her

lousy sense of judgment, as far as the big man beside her was concerned, it all came down to the bottom line.

Since increasing her bottom line was one of her new priorities, she took the hint and focused on it, too. Cynicism was new to her, but she could probably learn a lot from him.

"That would take more money than it's worth. I called him a month ago to let him know he was going to be a father. He wants nothing to do with me or the baby."

"What he wants doesn't matter. He has an obligation."

The edge had sharpened. Hearing it, her glance slid to his handsome profile. "Do you have a child?"

"No," he said, flatly. "I don't know anything about them, either," he admitted, sounding as if he planned to keep it that way. "But I do know that a man needs to accept his responsibilities if he does have one."

"That responsibility is something Geoff will fight and I can't afford to. The only money he said he'd give me was the cost of getting 'rid of it.' When I told him that wasn't going to happen, he said that even if I could prove it's his, the courts here have no jurisdiction over him. He also mentioned that I'd never be able to find him. His job there hadn't worked out and he was moving on."

The same awful disbelief she'd felt when she'd hung up from that call stabbed through her now. Afraid Max could see it, she focused on the vein in the bar top. That vein split in two. She felt like that a lot lately, as if the path she'd followed for so long had abruptly forked. Caught with no backup plan, she could only hope she was going in the right direction.

"Proving he's the father would be easy." She needed Max to know that, if for no other reason than to end the speculation in his heavy silence. "The only other man I've ever been with broke up with me three years ago. For not being spontaneous enough," she added, with a wry little laugh, "so it's not like there's any room for doubt. But I'm not going to waste energy or money on Geoff.

"I grew up without my dad," she admitted, fully aware of certain effects of her decision. "His dying was hardly his fault, but I hated him not being there. I've always felt that void in my life. But I don't want my child around a man who doesn't want her. I can't stand the thought of this baby ever feeling unwanted. That's why I'll do whatever I have to do to provide for her…and for my bistro," she added, "because this is how I'll take care of her. I just need to be able to hire an assistant."

She was willing to compromise to do that, too. She just needed the man avoiding her eyes to back down on cutting her employees' pay. They had responsibilities of their own. Now wasn't the time to remind him of that, though. Not only had she not yet uncovered whatever other surprises lurked in the papers he'd brought her, Alaina had just walked past the open kitchen door. Preoccupied with unwrapping her muffler, she hadn't seemed to notice them at the bar.

"Alaina is here," she murmured. Realizing the time, she grimaced. "Oh, geeze," she groaned. "I'm so sorry. You said you were in a hurry when you called." Apology magnified her disquiet as she tucked her hair into her clip and reached for her cap. "I hope I didn't make you late. I really didn't mean to keep you."

Max was certain she hadn't. He didn't doubt, either, that she felt as awkward about why she'd held him up as she did about all she'd just admitted.

She slid off the stool. With his own thoughts in check, he rose with her. "Are you okay now?" he asked, just to be sure she was steady on her feet.

"I am. And thank you…" For not looking at me as if

you think I've totally screwed up my life, she thought. Something that almost looked like compassion lurked in his eyes, along with a remoteness she found herself wanting badly to understand. "For helping me. And for this," she hurried to add, picking up the papers and envelope.

"Not a problem." Focused on the time, aware that he was going to be late, he took a step from her. Alaina had just stuck her head out the kitchen door. Looking as if she didn't want to interrupt, the waitress ducked back inside.

Now that someone else was there, he could leave.

More relieved by the reprieve than he wanted to admit, he nodded to the envelope. "Call after you've gone over that. There are a few things I know you'll have questions about."

Looking every bit as uneasy as he knew she felt, she told him she would and followed him to unlock the door and pull up the shade. As he walked out, the bistro lights flicked on, spilling brightness onto the sidewalk.

Her first customer was already hurrying toward the door as he rounded the front of his car. Since it was Friday, it occurred to him that Tommi could easily be there until midnight.

Max was the last person on the planet to tell anyone she worked too hard. He thrived on twelve-hour days. Fourteen was even better. But even he could see she was pushing herself to the limit to take care of her business, her employees, her customers and her neighbors. In the meantime, she was also doing what she had to do to make sure she could care for the child she apparently intended to raise on her own.

He'd known someone else like that. Someone who'd been abandoned by the man who'd gotten her pregnant and who'd worked as hard as she could to provide for her child. She'd struggled so hard and for so long that she'd literally worked herself into her grave.

The door on those memories slammed with the might of a gale-force wind. Tommi was not his mother. She had resources and skills his mother had not. Still, the sympathy he felt for her mingled with a sort of pity she'd probably hate knowing was there. Those telling feelings were just buried under a pile of defenses that brought the irrefutable need to walk away from what he shouldn't have to be dealing with at all.

If not for his partner, he wouldn't know a thing about her.

Allowing no further consideration than that, he pulled his cell phone from his pocket and opened his car door.

Starting the car, he keyed in "call me asap," and sent the message to Scott's cell phone.

He was on his way to his breakfast meeting when Scott called an hour later.

"Hey, man, I got the email Margie sent with the résumés you wanted me to look at. I know we need to hire a new office manager for Chicago if we're going to transfer Hochmeier to New York, but I just haven't had a chance to open it yet."

"That's not what I'm calling about."

The connection to India was as clear as lead crystal. Satellite technology at its best. The pause on the other end of the line sounded hugely relieved. "What's up, then?"

"Tommi Fairchild. How well do you know her?"

"Not as well as I'd like," he admitted bluntly. "Why?"

He'd told Scott a couple of days ago what Tommi had wanted when she'd agreed to the ill-fated meeting at the hotel. He'd also told him her operation had franchise possibilities, so he'd follow through on the preliminaries as he usually did, and that Scott could follow up with operating or construction changes. He hadn't exactly said that he'd be keeping the door open for him with her. But Scott had caught on, proclaimed him "the best," and insisted he owed him one.

If he'd been keeping track, his partner would realize he owed him more than that, but this wasn't about all the times Max had saved his butt over the years.

"Are you sure you're serious about her?" he asked.

"As serious about a woman as I've ever been. Is there a problem?"

The guy hadn't even hesitated.

"Not for me. Investment-wise, her business is definitely smaller than we'd normally look at, but the profit potential is there." That was his focus. Or so he wanted to believe. "I just think you might be getting in deeper than you realize."

The laugh that came through the phone's tiny speaker was quick and easygoing. "Since when did you start worrying about my love life, partner? First, you offer to help me out. Now you're warning me away?"

"Just doing my due diligence. You know I like all the facts up front."

"So what facts do you think I need to know?"

"Just one. She's pregnant."

The laugh died.

After a few rather long moments, Max thought the connection had died, too.

"Hey. Are you there?"

"Yeah. Yeah," Scott repeated, apparently mulling the little drawback. "Pregnant, huh? Where's the daddy?"

"Gone."

Silence gathered again. When the ex–college linebacker spoke again his affable tone was back. "You didn't get a reputation for being hard-ass thorough for nothing, did you, Callahan? Thanks for the heads-up."

It was Max's turn to pause. "No problem. Just wanted to know if you were still interested."

"I am. Definitely."

Max didn't hear a trace of doubt in his partner's tone, nothing at all to indicate that the little bombshell he'd just dropped had given him anything more than a few moments pause. That didn't seem anything like the man he knew, the man who made it a rule to never date a woman two weeks in a row so she wouldn't get serious. But then, nothing about his partner and Tommi Fairchild made any sense. Not to him.

"This might change my approach," he heard Scott admit, "but I'm still in the game. Keep the ball rolling with her, okay? I'll be back next week. And about those résumés," he went on, shifting gears with the ease of a race-car driver, "it might be a while before I get to them. Gray wants to close on one of the properties here. I'm going to be tied up for a while."

Since HuntCom was one of their biggest accounts, he told him he was glad to hear that. That their commission would be in the two-million range also softened any irritation he might have felt over yet another delay with staffing the so far nonexistent East Coast branch. Moments later, he ended the call as he aimed for the freeway on-ramp.

The status of their own business wasn't what had mattered to him, anyway. He'd just wanted to know if Scott was still interested in pursuing the woman. Since he hadn't let himself think about why he'd wanted to know that before he'd texted him, now that he knew how truly infatuated his partner was, he wasn't going to think about it now, either. He would just handle her account the way he would any other—and stuff down the protectiveness he didn't want right along with everything else he didn't want to feel for her, anyway.

If there was anything Max could do, it was block what he didn't want to deal with. After all, he'd had a lifetime of practice. Yet, whether he wanted to acknowledge it or not, that protectiveness was still there, along with all of his defenses, when he returned to the bistro after Tommi's call two days later.

Chapter Six

The cold drizzle that had leaked from the gray sky all Sunday morning was taking a break when Max parked in front of the bistro. From the looks of the wreath on a large, red storage box under its domed green awning and the ladder nearby, Tommi had decided to use the undoubtedly brief respite to put up Christmas decorations.

She just didn't appear to be anywhere around.

Since the bistro was closed for the day, Max headed for the corner of the redbrick building to go around back, passing a row of two-foot-high faux fir trees on his way. They occupied the long iron planter box below the arching gold *THE CORNER BISTRO* stenciled on the large front window.

When he'd been there a couple of days ago, the planter had overflowed with some sort of flowers in yellow and rust.

Twenty feet ahead, he saw Tommi poke her head around the corner of the building.

She'd heard a vehicle slow on the wet pavement, heard the slam of a door after it stopped. Seeing Max walk from the expensive black Mercedes that hadn't been there minutes ago, her heart gave a funny little jump.

He had his hands tucked into the front pockets of his casual cords. The stance pulled back the sides of the heavy squall jacket that made his shoulders look huge, and exposed the crew-neck sweater stretched over his hard chest. He looked very large, very male and despite his faint smile when he saw her, very preoccupied.

To her relief, no mention had been made of how she'd wound up in his arms when they'd talked briefly on the phone Friday afternoon, and nothing he'd said indicated any misgivings about continuing to do business with her.

Her own uncertainties about the partnership had compounded, though.

"I'll just be a minute," she called. One of the clauses in the proposal he'd left dealt with putting their own manager on-site. He assured her that the proposal simply covered all the bases and that the point was negotiable. Still, its existence added another stress to the awkwardness and anxiety she felt now that he was here. "I should have had these up last weekend."

With the nod of his dark head and his distracted, "No rush," she went back to lining up faux trees in the planter below the window on the park side of her bistro. She didn't want to keep him waiting, but she really needed to finish what she'd put off far longer than she should have.

This would be her third Christmas since she'd opened the restaurant. The two years before, she'd plunged headfirst into the joy of the season and changed the decor from "fall" to "holiday" over Thanksgiving weekend. With her life totally upended, joy missing, the task simply hadn't been a priority.

For a number of reasons, she made it a priority now. She didn't want to cheat her customers of the sparkle and cheer of a holiday atmosphere. Or her neighbors. Or her staff. She especially didn't want one of her sisters or her mom dropping by and wondering why her decorations weren't up.

"Looks nice."

Max had rounded the corner.

"Thanks," she murmured, stressed enough without the unnerving way his glance slid over her. In the space of seconds, his assessing blue eyes moved from the scrunchie holding her high ponytail in place, to her cocoa-colored parka and down the length of her jeans. Since she hadn't been able to zip up her favorite pair that morning, she was wearing her fat ones; the pair that, under other circumstances, would have had her ruthlessly cutting carbs until her skinnier ones fit again. It seemed as if she'd thickened around her waist almost overnight.

She could have sworn his glance lingered on her middle.

She stepped back from the planter. Trying not to worry about whatever he was thinking, she frowned at the middle tree in the compact row of seven.

Max walked up behind her, looked over the top of her head.

"The middle one needs to go left."

She could almost feel his heat radiating into her back. Too conscious of him, definitely not needing the way his nearness toyed with her nerves, she moved back to the window.

She edged the little tree to one side, adjusted the one next to it.

"Better," he concluded.

"Thanks," she murmured.

"What else do you need to do out here?" he asked. "Unless you need your notes, we can talk while we do it."

She had far more color than when he'd last seen her. Her cheeks were pinked by the cold breeze, her unadorned mouth was the color of a blush. Her eyes looked tired to him, though. Bothered by the latter, not questioning why, Max focused on the caution lifting from those dark depths. Even as it relieved him to see her smile forming, he reminded himself he was there to close a deal. He might as well get it done as quickly as possible.

"Thanks, but I wouldn't want to impose."

"You wouldn't be. I'm here, anyway."

The delicate wing of one eyebrow arched. "Is that the two-birds-with-one-stone approach to negotiating?"

"Whatever works," he replied, his shrug tight.

His offer was a two-edged sword. Helping her outside while they discussed the issues they needed to address seemed infinitely preferable to being with her in the confines of her empty bistro. On the other hand, the last thing he wanted was to get involved in a decorating thing. The entire holiday season was something he didn't so much ignore as he did endure. He didn't have the luxury of ignoring it. There were too many parties to attend and too many clients to remember with gifts and cards and whatever else Margie reminded him needed to be done to pretend the season didn't exist. So he simply tolerated it instead, and used it as a marketing tool.

"If you're willing," Tommi conceded, "that would be great. I usually put lights around the windows. The little white ones like those," she said, motioning to the pre-wrapped lights on the fake firs. "But I'd been thinking about just going with 'simple' this year." The savings to her personal energy aside, she'd thought it would be pretty enough with the lights on the little trees reflecting on the windows at night.

But pretty enough wasn't as pretty as it could be.

She didn't care at all for the idea of doing less than her best.

"If you were a customer here," she prefaced, "which would you rather see? Understated decorations, or more festive ones?"

"I'm not the right person to ask."

Tommi opened her mouth, closed it again. Considering his list of opinions about the rest of her operation, she had trouble believing that he'd go mute on something so visible. "But you eat out," she reminded him as they started around the corner. "Do you think people feel something is missing if decorations are subtle?"

"It depends on how they feel about this time of year. Some people probably want all the…trappings," he called them. "Some people don't."

The breeze blew a loose strand of hair across her cheek. Tipping her head so the wind could blow it back, she glanced over to see that he still had his hands jammed into his pockets. His left hand jingled his keys. Despite his conversational tone, there seemed to be a hint of defensiveness in his voice. That same subtle guard etched his profile as she stopped short of the bistro's front door.

He was one of those people who wished Christmas would disappear. She felt that as surely as she did her own disconnect from the season now. She just had no idea how long his aversion had existed.

"I wasn't thinking of how difficult this time of year can be for some people." She'd been so caught up in her scramble to regain her sense of security that she'd considered little beyond what was required of her. "I know what you mean, though. I had a hard time with holidays for a long time, too.

"I was ten when my dad died," she said, since he already knew she'd grown up without him. "Before that, I remember Christmas being this wonderful sense of anticipation with parties and lights…" *And feeling utterly safe in that little world,* she thought. "For a long time after, Mom went through the motions for us, but it was never the same.

"It took a long time to really look forward to the holidays," she admitted, picking up a wreath from atop the plastic tub of lights. "But seeing everyone else happy made me happy, too. So, the spirit did come back. Just in a different way."

Lifting the wreath to the chalkboard mounted between the front door and the window, she hung it on the little hook above it. The words on the board, *Welcome to The Corner Bistro,* weren't actually written on it in chalk. She'd just had them painted to look that way.

With the greeting now encircled in noble fir and pine, she turned to meet the quiet curiosity in his otherwise guarded features.

"I'm sorry about whatever it was that took the joy out of the season for you, Max. If whatever it is was recent, or if this time of year is still difficult, please don't think you need to help with any of this. I'll quit now and we can go inside."

He'd stopped toying with his keys, but the guard in his expression remained as he considered her. "It stopped being difficult a long time ago. I just look at it all now as a way to maintain client contacts." He nodded toward the box beside her. "Just tell me what you want me to do."

She'd all but asked him to open up to her. At least a little. She truly didn't want to overstep herself, and she certainly didn't want to make a potentially recent hurt worse. She just needed badly to know more about him.

Even without the need to know who she might be going into business with, she would have wanted to know what memory of his home had brought the quick distance about him the other day, and why he'd been so adamant about a man's obligation to support his child when he'd just as clearly not liked the idea of having children himself. She wanted to know, too, why she sensed such restlessness in him. And what made him so inherently kind, yet so closed and inaccessible.

She wanted to know if he ever felt the need to let someone in.

"I'm sorry about your father," he said, but gave her nothing else.

The breeze picked up the scent of fresh pine from the wreath, scattered curled leaves down the wet sidewalk. With the tails of the red ribbon on the ring of greenery fluttering behind Tommi, Max watched the sympathy in her expression give way to apology for having bumped into something obviously uncomfortable for him. There was something more there, too. He just wouldn't let himself wonder what it was as she murmured, "Thank you," and turned away.

Her perception had caught him completely off guard. So had her concern for him. Not sure what to make of either, or how to take away the quick unease he'd caused her to feel, he settled for dismissing the concern as inconsequential and tried to ignore the rest.

"If you don't mind, you can help me put lights around the windows."

Thinking she looked more tired, and more wary, than she probably realized, he looked up. The top of the window was only nine feet or so from the sidewalk. Not far, but too far to stretch. "I don't mind. You shouldn't be on a ladder, anyway."

"Why not?"

Max's expression remained utterly unreadable to Tommi. So did his glance as it slid to where her jacket covered her stomach.

"You just shouldn't." A frown finally surfaced. "How do you hang those things?"

"On the clips. They're inside the frame. But wait a minute," she said, catching his arm as he started past her.

Conscious of how the muscle in his jaw jerked when he met her eyes, she pulled away her hand. She didn't step back, though, not even from his odd displeasure. Though the street was all but deserted, she didn't want her voice to carry on the chill breeze.

"I'm only pregnant," she murmured, afraid her condition was influencing him after all. "It's not like a disease or a disability, Max. I can do everything I usually do. I told you the other day that I'll keep up all the things I've always done here. I meant that."

"I wasn't insinuating that you couldn't keep up."

The woman was determined to a fault. Stubborn, too. But what he saw in her gentle features looked too vulnerable for him to believe it was just her independence driving her.

"I was only thinking that you look pretty tired, and that you might not want to fall." He hated that she kept stressing so much. It couldn't possibly be good for her. "The ladder is wet and your soles are leather. Mine aren't."

Her glance fell to their feet. Her boots were suede with a stylish little heel. His heftier ones were made for hiking. He was just being logical, she realized. And thoughtful. The way he had been at the hotel. And the other day when he'd stayed close so he could catch her again if she fell.

He was looking out for her.

That realization touched her in ways she knew she shouldn't let matter, but mattered far too much, anyway.

"Just for the record," he added, "I have no doubt that you'll continue pushing to do everything you do. Stop worrying. Okay?"

His phrasing lent an odd edge to his assurance. But that assurance was all she cared about just then.

"Does that mean you'll drop the on-site manager clause?" she asked.

The edge faded.

"We'll drop it," he agreed. "We'll go with a modified silent partnership."

"Modified?"

"Come on. Hand me some lights before it starts raining again," he said. "We'll talk while we get them up.

"By modifying," he explained, climbing the ladder as she unwound the string of clear lights, "I mean the company will take our agreed-on forty percent interest in your business in return for paying for the expansion. For the first year, we'll also pay all salaries, including the new chef's." He took the string she handed him, turned to the window. "You'll retain full creative and managerial control and send us monthly reports, but we'll set caps on salaries and insurance."

Her sixty percent left her with controlling interest. That part was huge. It was the part she couldn't control that bothered her. "I'm still not comfortable with cutting pay and benefits."

Arms stretched above him, he slipped the string into the clips under the high window frame. "I know you're not. And I know it's hard for you not to be generous," he admitted, his tone utterly patient. "But that generosity is what prevented you from qualifying for a loan and having to go with a partnership instead."

"I wasn't being generous." The realization that he was looking out for her lingered. So did the undeniable draw of that knowledge. Yet, the hard-core businessman in him clearly didn't allow him to see what seemed so apparent to her. "I was just being fair."

"You can't afford to be that 'fair,'" he pointed out, then asked for another string of lights.

Since she couldn't effectively argue his logic, she didn't try. She just handed him what he'd asked for, then took over clipping the string down the side of the frame and along the bottom of the window behind the trees when he got to where she could reach it herself.

"Does the franchise clause have to stay?" Surely that could go, she thought. The only bistro she wanted was the one she had now.

"You want that clause," he assured her. "Franchising can make you a wealthy woman."

"I don't need to be wealthy," she insisted, wondering if it was his expression or her nerves that seemed a little tight when she reached the side of the window and he took over. "I just need to earn enough for me and my baby to be comfortable."

"You'll be more comfortable with a bigger nest egg. And, probably," he muttered, his back to her, "a bigger nest."

She already had plans to move to the two-bedroom apartment down the hall. When she told him that, his response was to meet her eyes, shake his head at what he apparently considered her lack of grander foresight, snap in the last light and say, "What's next?"

She told him they needed to do the window on the side.

"Then, what about the lease on the space next door?"

she asked, moving on to the expansion as they carried box and ladder around the corner. "Do you deal with that or do I?"

"Our office will take care of it."

He set the ladder in place, climbed up. With him near the top rung, her eyes were even with his boots as she held up lights. "And the contractor?"

"Scott will handle that," he said over the tick of tiny bulbs bumping glass. "You'll just need to oversee the design."

Scott. She kept forgetting about him. She hadn't forgotten the information he'd imparted about his partner, though, spare as it had been.

"He called yesterday." Just after she'd removed his roses from the bar because they'd started to fade. "He wanted to make sure all my questions were being answered, and to tell me to call him if there was anything I didn't understand."

What he'd actually said was that he wanted to make sure his partner was treating her right, and that she shouldn't let Max's workaholic tendencies intimidate her. According to him, Max often forgot that the rest of the world didn't live, eat and breathe expansions and acquisitions. He'd assured her he'd be back toward the end of the week. Then, the two of them could start working together.

She wasn't especially looking forward to that. Probably, she thought, because the man still sounded interested in pursuing her along with her business. Yet, he was part of the company to which a huge part of herself would soon belong. It only made sense to know more about him.

Since she'd mentioned Scott, Max hadn't said a thing as he continued tackling her chore for her.

"Does he have family here?"

He gave the string a tug. "A stepmother."

The loose end of the string had caught on one of the little fir trees. She unsnagged it. "Did he lose his father, too?"

The lights seemed to tick against the glass more sharply.

"Years ago."

"Are they close?"

"Who?"

"Your partner and his stepmother."

"Not especially," he muttered, sounding as if he might be understating considerably.

"Does he have other family?"

Looking up, she saw the underside of his strong jaw tighten.

"If you have questions about Scott, you'll have to ask him."

"Then, what about you? Do you have family here?"

From his hesitation, it seemed he didn't like that question, either.

"No, I don't," he said and clipped in two more lights.

"They must be in Los Angeles, then."

He aimed a frown at her upturned face. "Why do you think that?"

"Your website said you earned your MBA at UCLA. I thought maybe you grew up there."

"I grew up in a lot of places."

"So you have family in different cities?"

He'd reached the end of the string. Or, maybe, it was his rope. With his frown deepening the creases in his forehead, he climbed down the ladder and took the bundle of lights she held. Once that was strung they'd be finished.

The almost comfortable ease they'd managed as they'd worked on the front window had vanished like smoke in the wind.

"Are you using the back door or the front?" he asked, totally ignoring her question.

"Back."

"I'll put these up. You take the box inside and I'll bring the ladder. It's starting to rain."

It seemed to Tommi that there was nothing quite so deafening as the sound of a slammed door. Especially when standing right in front of it.

It was barely raining at all. Just a few little drops that hardly qualified as a sprinkle, much less anything requiring escape.

Escape from her was clearly what he wanted as he turned away. From her questions, anyway.

He just as clearly expected her to take the hint.

The man had no idea how tenacious she could be when she really wanted something.

"You did the high parts," she reminded him, taking the lights back to finish them up herself. "I can do the rest. And, by the way, I've answered every question you've asked me." Clips snapped as she secured green wire. "You know everything about me from my checking account balance to something my family doesn't even know."

"I need to know who we're doing business with," he defended.

"So do I," she defended, right back. "I need to know who I'm doing business with, too."

She glanced around to see a muscle in his jaw jerk. She had a point and he knew it. He didn't like that she had one, either. She just couldn't begin to imagine why that was.

Looking caught, not liking it, he finally conceded.

"What do you want to know?"

"About your family," she said, trying not to sound exasperated. "About where you're from." *About your personal life, or if you even have one,* she thought. "Something that tells me who you are besides a fabulously successful investor who tracks down properties for big corporations."

Max wasn't sure if the twitch at the corner of his mouth was a smile or a grimace. He liked the compliment. He liked the way her frustration with him animated her expression. What he didn't care for at all was how she kept walking all over the graveyard of a past he'd laid to rest long ago.

"It's actually the other way around. The investment part is a sideline."

It seemed to be all she could do not to roll her eyes. Exasperation fairly leaked from her fine pores.

"As for the rest of it," he conceded, keeping it simple, "my mother is dead, I never knew my father and I have no idea what family is supposed to be." The whole concept had eluded him. He knew nothing of how that dynamic worked. "If it's blood relatives you're talking about, I imagine I have them somewhere, but I don't know who they are. As for anyone else who might have once qualified, I had a wife who left after six months about twenty years ago. I grew up in Nevada and Southern California. Scott has always lived in Washington," he added, since she was, rightfully, entitled to background on both of them, "but like I said before, you'll have to ask him about the rest of it."

Tommi was still focused on what he'd said about his parents. And his wife. From the sounds of it, he'd been abandoned in one way or another by the very people who could well have mattered to him the most.

She also had the feeling she now understood why he'd been so adamant about a man's obligation to his offspring. His father had also abandoned his mother and left her to raise him alone.

"You said you grew up in lots of places," she quietly reminded him. "What kind of work did your mother do?"

Of all the things she could have asked, Max hadn't seen that one coming. The women who'd prodded him about his past inevitably asked about his ex.

"She cleaned."

"Cleaned?"

"Hotel rooms during the day. Offices at night. For a while, she cleaned private houses. It depended on what kind of agency hired her."

"Why did you move so much?"

"Because she was looking for a way out." He realized that now, though he hadn't at the time. "We moved to Las Vegas because she heard the casino hotels paid more." It had been the same for Tahoe. "When that didn't work—" for reasons he'd never known and never asked "—we moved…somewhere else," he concluded, because he really didn't want to think about the homeless shelters they'd stayed in on occasion, too.

What he would never forget, though, was what he'd glimpsed of how others had lived. When she'd been afraid to leave him alone, his mom had snuck him inside some of the casino hotel rooms and the houses she'd cleaned while the owners were away. No doubt that was what had gotten her fired on more than one occasion.

It was what he wasn't saying that Tommi heard. His mother hadn't had many options. She worked hard and for not much money. She'd done what she had to do.

She'd been looking for a way out, he'd said.

"Was she very young?" she asked, realizing that she might well have been.

The same distance she'd sensed in him the other day suddenly threatened to lock into place. "She was sixteen when she had me. She had to drop out of school."

"And the woman you married?" she ventured, wanting to change the direction of his thoughts even as her own remained on his mom. Sixteen was still a child. And she'd been alone with a child of her own. "You said she left?"

"We shouldn't have married in the first place."

Though he offered the admission grudgingly, it was easier to talk about his ex. He figured he owed Tommi at least as much as she'd given him, anyway. It couldn't have been easy for her to confide that what had happened with her child's father should never have happened at all. He was painfully familiar with that sort of guilt-inducing hindsight, but at least he wasn't having to live with any life-changing consequences.

"We were young. After Mom died, I didn't have anybody and Jenna didn't seem to, either. Three months after our trip to the justice of the peace, her old boyfriend decided he wanted her back." She hadn't needed Max anymore. End of story. "It was as much my fault it didn't work as it was hers."

"You're very generous," Tommi murmured.

"I'm not being generous." He wasn't about to take that sort of credit. Not from her. He didn't deserve it. "Marrying her had just been a way to make sure she stayed with me. Obviously, that rationale proved flawed."

His cynicism didn't surprise Tommi. Neither did the way he brushed right over the admission of how very alone he must have felt, and how badly he'd wanted a connection to someone—to someone who was family.

It was no wonder he didn't like the holidays. The people who would have made them special were gone.

"How old were you when you lost your mom?"

"Eighteen. Look," he muttered. He'd gone far enough. He had no desire to revisit the months he'd taken care of his mom after she'd come down with pneumonia and become too sick to work. Or, with how he'd struggled after she'd died to find places to live while he put himself through school. He especially didn't like the inexplicable feeling that considering all that was exactly what he should do, though he had no idea what purpose it could possibly serve.

"It's raining. We should get this stuff inside and finish working out the agreement. I know you want to get back to the guy you want to hire as soon as you can."

It finally had started to rain, heavily enough that Tommi flipped up the hood of her jacket as she grabbed the now-empty storage tub. She wasn't sure if she felt chastised by the abrupt way he'd closed the door on something he clearly hadn't intended to share, or bad for the pain those memories must have once caused.

He wasn't a man who invited sympathy. Still, as he collapsed the ladder and they headed for the alley and the bistro's back door, she knew how lost she would feel without the familial connections that sometimes drove her crazy. Because of that, it wasn't hard to imagine how awful it would be to live without a connection to any family at all.

She pushed back her hood as they walked inside. "I'll take that," she said, reaching for the ladder.

"Just tell me where you want it."

"I need it so I can put this back up on the shelf."

She'd lifted the red plastic container.

He promptly took it from her.

"I've got it. Just tell me where you want it."

His tone might have sounded casual if not for the faintly clipped edge to it. Just as conscious of the subtle restiveness in his manner, she motioned quickly to the small utility room. As he turned into the neatly organized space, she backed into the deserted and thoroughly scrubbed kitchen.

The only sounds in the room were the rattle of the ladder

bumping the mop bucket Mario had used last night when they'd cleaned up. The scents of cleaner and bleach still lingered. Grabbing a clean white hand towel from the stack on a metal rack, she held it out to Max the moment he turned from the little room.

What she wanted to do was tell him she hadn't meant to pry as deeply as she had. Fairly certain he'd rather she let it go, she sought more comfortable ground herself.

"You're wet," she said, looking from the rain beaded on his squall jacket to the droplets clinging to his dark hair.

Max watched her lift the towel a little higher, saw a tentative smile enter her eyes.

"The papers are out on the bar. Dry off and I'll get you some coffee."

That little smile held apology and what almost looked like concern. Bracing himself against the appealing curve of her mouth, he took what she held. "Don't go to the trouble."

"It's no trouble. I have everything ready. All I need to do is pour the water into the pot. Besides, it was cold out there. This will warm you."

She knew he liked French press. So that was what she had set out to prepare for him.

"I have a couple servings of pear torte left," she told him, unzipping her jacket. She had one of bread pudding, too, though she wasn't about to offer him that. "Do you want some with your coffee?"

"You don't have to wait on me, Tommi. Or feed me. And regular coffee would have been fine."

"But you like this kind better," she reminded him.

That was beside the point. "Tommi, don't." He didn't want her doing anything special for him. He didn't want her feeling sorry about his aversion for a holiday he hadn't cele-brated since he was seventeen. He didn't want her looking at him with all that concern, or making him want to know if her mouth was as soft as it looked. He didn't want to remember the incredible silkiness of her hair, her skin or how perfect she'd felt in his arms.

Mostly, he didn't want the restlessness that came with wondering what she'd feel like naked and moving beneath him.

He pushed his fingers through his damp hair, his body tight with the unfamiliar and building frustration he had to jam down every time he was with her.

"You don't need to take care of me the way you do everyone else around here. You have enough to do as it is," he muttered, trying hard not to sound as defensive as he suddenly felt. "Let's just get this agreement ironed out. Or, better yet," he decided, since his effort seemed to be failing, "call me tomorrow and we can go over the rest of it on the phone. We should have everything wrapped up by the end of the week."

She set the small pot back on the workstation. As she did, the faint click of metal bumping metal merged with the no-nonsense ring of his cell phone.

Tommi watched him pull it from his pocket. After a quick glance to see who was calling, he palmed it and let the call go to voice mail.

"If you'd rather I call, of course I'll do that." His edginess had escalated. She could practically feel it humming along her skin.

That feeling lingered as he gave her a tight smile, and an even tighter nod.

"Tomorrow, then," he said—and left her with the strange feeling that he hadn't closed her out, so much as he'd closed himself in.

Chapter Seven

Max leaned against the edge of his wide, ebony desk, his jaw tight and his arms crossed over his loosened silk tie. On the other side of his expansive office with its built-in bar and insanely expensive modern art, Scott adjusted the lens on the telescope in front of the wall of windows. Their 40th floor offices afforded sweeping views of Puget Sound and the islands and peninsula beyond, but he wouldn't be able to see much through the fog and drizzle.

His brawny, fair-haired partner wasn't interested in the view, anyway. He was just trying to let him know he took the problem less seriously than Max did.

"I know you want to open that office the first of March, Max. And I know it could take a while to work in the right people. What's the big deal if we push it to June? Or even wait a year?" he asked, abandoning the non-view to poke through the files stacked on the conference table. "We've been doing great working out of here and Chicago."

"The 'big deal' is that we could be doing even better if we were bigger."

"And to get bigger means one of us is going to have even less time than he does now. Since you already sleep in your suit, that means it's my time getting cut into."

"Since you only work three days a week that shouldn't be a problem."

The tips of Scott's ears reddened as he looked up. "I just spent ten days in Singapore closing the HuntCom deal."

"And the two weeks before that in the Florida Keys."

"Is it my fault you don't take vacations?"

"You spent the first of November on some game shoot. That left you all of three days in Chicago and five here last month."

"You're keeping track of my time?"

It was all Max could do to keep his resentment in check. "We have clients, Scott. Somebody has to take the meetings."

His jaw worked as he took a deep breath. They'd been through this before. In the past year, past two, probably, Scott had taken "down time" to a whole new level.

"You agreed to expand," he pointed out, ever so tightly.

"Well, I changed my mind. I don't want to move to New York."

Because of Tommi, Max thought. "Fine," he said. "I will."

"That still leaves everything here to me!" He checked his own tone. "Maybe I don't want to work that hard."

Clearly ready to move on, Scott returned his attention to the files. "Let's just get to what we need to do here, okay? Bring me up to speed on the Westland and SymTech relocations." He nudged at another file, checked the tab. "And

The Corner Bistro." Picking the file up, he smiled. "Let's start with this one."

Max's frustration with his partner suddenly collided with agitation of an entirely different sort. He'd done his best not to think about the woman with the warm brown eyes who scraped at his raw spots and drew him with her smile. She had called on Monday, as they'd agreed, but he hadn't seen her since he'd helped her hang her lights. Now, every time he saw Christmas lights, he thought of her. And Christmas lights were everywhere.

Pushing his hands into his pockets, feeling restless, he paced toward the tall curve of polished marble anchoring one end of his credenza. "She's fine with everything except the clause about wages and insurance. I reminded her that our agreement with our investors is for a certain percentage of profit. For our company to do business with her, the clause has to stay. She agreed." Ever so reluctantly, he remembered. "So legal messengered the final contract over to her yesterday. It's pretty much the standard agreement for a silent partnership we have with the other restaurants in the portfolio."

"I wish you hadn't sent the contract out. I could have taken it to her myself."

Remaining silent, Max kept his back to where he could hear Scott flipping through her file.

"I called her when I got back last night," his partner continued, sounding faintly distracted by what he was perusing. "I told her I wanted to talk about her expansion, but she said she's really busy right now. Something about private dinner parties she needs to prepare for. I think I'll stop by, anyway. Just tell her I'm checking to make sure she's okay with everything, you know?"

Mention of the private dinner parties she had booked had Max frowning at the large oval of rock. He didn't care what Tommi had said about her energy coming back soon. She needed it now. He could only imagine how exhausted she'd be by the time the holidays were over.

"We need to take good care of her. Really good care," Scott emphasized, oblivious to his partner's silence. "That girl is a goldmine."

Max turned, his frown firmly in place. "What are you talking about? Her operation is the smallest we've ever taken on."

"It's her connections, man." With his golden-boy grin, Scott tossed the file onto the table. "I've only met her once. A little over a month ago at some event for the Hunt Foundation.

"Harry was telling me he'd heard great things about our operation and started asking all kinds of personal questions. He's kind of eccentric, you know," he added with an easy chuckle, "so I just went along with what he asked and pretty soon he'd had her brought over. He introduced her as his surrogate niece and a member of his board of directors. After she left, he hinted pretty heavily that there could be a position on his board for me if I got serious about her."

He shook his head, grinning. "Guess he's looking to make an honest woman out of her before she has her kid. He didn't mention that she was in a family way," he stressed, sounding as if he figured the guy had deliberately withheld that bit of information. "But, hey. She's easy enough on the eyes." He set aside the file he apparently intended to take with him. "And I imagine she has one hell of a trust fund."

Glancing back, looking like an ad for weekend wear, he planted his hands on the hips of his casual slacks.

His smile did a slow fade.

"What?" he asked.

With questions piling up like cars in a chain collision,

Max didn't bother to question the protectiveness that had risen straight up his back. His expression ominous, his tone more so, his eyes narrowed to slits of blue ice.

"Tommi knows Harry Hunt?"

"I just said she did. She's on his board—"

"I got that." He'd also understood that Harry had introduced her as a surrogate niece, whatever that meant. What he didn't understand was why Tommi would have come to them if she had ties to the Hunts. "And I finally get why you're after her. I just don't believe what I'm hearing. You just want to use her?"

Scott held up his hands, palms out, his expression appeasing. "Let's not put it that way," he countered easily. "Men marry women all the time for what they can do for them and their careers. Who knows what doors she can open for me?" He held his hands wide. "And for you," he pointed out, ever generous. "The company will benefit, too. If all this works out and we start getting business from Harry's Forbes-list buddies, you'll have all the expansion you can handle. Just hire more help."

Max wasn't sure if the man was looking for support, approval or a blessing. Whichever it was, he wasn't getting it from him. The fact that he didn't seem to think Max would be at all put off by his ploy felt like an insult.

"You know what, Layman?" Disgust fairly dripped from Max's tone. "I've overlooked little things like you working half as hard for half our profits—"

"Hey," the beefier man cut in. "It's not half as hard. Just because you've had to cover a few meetings for me lately—"

"I'm not going to debate your math skills," Max shot back. "If you can't make a meeting, you figure out how to explain it to the client. I'm done covering for you."

Clearly trying to defuse him, obviously thinking it was

only his work habits ticking off his partner, Scott's easygoing smile resurfaced. "Come on, man. You know you'll do what you have to do to make all this work. You love this company too much to let me mess it up."

The good-natured, every-guy's-buddy attitude worked well with everyone else. It used to work with Max, too, mostly because Max didn't tend to sweat the small stuff in their working relationship. But the small stuff had become bigger with his partner's blatant disregard for his responsibilities.

It had become huge with what he had revealed about the reasons he'd staked his claim on Tommi.

The deceptive calm remained in Max's voice. It was the steel threading it that added the threatening edge. "I care about it." The company was as much his life as Tommi's bistro was hers. "But I meant what I said. If you have a meeting, you show up. You pull your weight. And as far as Tommi Fairchild is concerned, the last thing she needs is you or anyone else trying to manipulate her. Stay away from her bistro."

At the purely masculine warning, good nature failed. "Hey, buddy. You need to remember who owned this company first. You wouldn't be a partner here if I hadn't hired you on. My end of these deals is to implement any physical changes we're paying for. I'll oversee her expansion. Whatever I want with her personally is none of your business."

Heat rising from the collar of his polo shirt, he glanced away, looked right back. As if he'd just caught the possessiveness in Max's tone, his eyes narrowed.

"Are you after her yourself?"

A corded muscle pulsed in Max's neck. "The only thing I'm after is for you to stop screwing around. We don't abuse our business relationships. And what you need to remember," he echoed in the man's same posturing tone, "is that you wouldn't still have this operation if I hadn't come on board." He'd have played it right into the ground. "Unless you want me to get her on the phone right now so you can tell her why you're after her, you leave her alone."

Scott clearly took exception to having his hand called. He didn't look too happy having his plans with his little goldmine gutted, either. But with no way to defend himself and his calculating now worthless, he seemed to think better of voicing any further displeasure in the moments before a knock sounded on the door.

The instant it opened, Margie poked her head inside.

"Sorry to interrupt, gentlemen," she said, her neat gray bob swinging. "But, Scott, Kathy said you wanted to know when the box of documents you shipped from Singapore arrived. FedEx just left. She put them in your office.

"Max," she continued, all quick, professional efficiency as she walked in and slipped his mail into the inbox on his spreadsheet-covered desk, "Ross Hayden has called twice in the past hour. He said he spoke with you last week about moving their operation to Washington from San Jose. He wants to meet with you as soon as possible.

"I made your reservations for Chicago on Monday," she went on, seeming aware of the tension in the room, clearly intent on ignoring it. "If you want to tack that trip on, let me know and I'll route you from Chicago to San Jose. It's only two weeks until Christmas and flights are filling up."

The interruption had Max drawing a deep breath. "I'll do that," he told her. "Thanks."

He'd call their client now, he thought, turning to his desk. He had nothing else to say to his partner, anyway. With Scott avoiding eye contact with him as he followed his assistant out, it seemed apparent he didn't have anything to add to their discussion, either.

He wasn't sure he trusted the resentment in his partner's

silence. Or if he trusted his partner anymore at all for that matter. More pressing just then was that he had no idea what was going on with the woman who was working so hard to take care of the business and the people she cared about.

He wanted to know why she hadn't gone to Harry Hunt for the money she needed to pay her new chef. The man was as rich as Croesus. What she needed would be the equivalent of pennies to him.

He wanted to know what she was doing on the board of directors of a multibillion-dollar international computer corporation.

He especially wanted to know why Harry Hunt was trying to marry her off, and offering bribes in the process. Scott had assumed that the man wanted to legitimize her baby, possibly even save face for her. But Max didn't believe her pregnancy was the reason at all. She was trying too hard to keep that circumstance to herself. As far as he knew, he—and his partner—were the only ones who knew she was expecting.

He jammed his fingers through his hair. The fact that he'd somehow thought he was protecting his partner by disclosing her condition now seemed laughable. Even as the thought registered, so did guilt. When he'd made that call, he'd also wanted to know if the information would change his partner's interest in her. Now, as then, he didn't question why that had mattered. All he considered was that Scott wouldn't have been privy to the fact if not for him. Tommi hadn't asked him not to say anything about her condition. Yet, he felt as if he'd betrayed her, anyway.

He stood behind his desk, his hands on his hips, head down, jaw working. The questions demanded answers. The disgust, disappointment and protectiveness coiling inside him demanded that he step back and wait. He didn't trust anything about what he felt just then. Least of all the intensity of it. Because of that, he wouldn't allow himself to pick up the phone and call her. He'd hear from her as soon as she finished reviewing the final contract, anyway. Though she'd agreed to its terms, knowing her, she'd try one last time to talk him out of the wage clause.

Having decided that much, Max started to make the call to their new client only to be interrupted by another call. Then, by Margie needing signatures. Then, by Scott, all business, wanting to know when he'd be available to talk about the WestLand properties. He'd decided to take a long weekend and go skiing, so the sooner the better.

The fact that the unmistakably disgruntled guy would soon be off to play again suited Max just fine. With him gone for a few days, he didn't need to worry just yet about what sort of payback his partner had in mind.

Most of the interruptions, though, were from the questions that continued to nag him as he paced a trough in the carpet of his penthouse two days later.

When Max finally picked up the phone at nine-thirty Sunday morning, he was on his tenth trip between the black lacquer and stainless steel of his rarely used kitchen and the long wall of windows overlooking the rain-grayed sound. Turning his back on the view he'd paid a small fortune to own, he punched in Tommi's home number.

He hadn't wanted to call her at the bistro. He'd known she'd be busy. With others inevitably around, she wouldn't have been free to talk, anyway. Since the bistro was closed for the day, and it still being relatively early, he figured now was as good a time as any to get his questions answered.

Or so he was thinking when he heard the mechanical click of her answering machine and Tommi's recorded voice saying, "Hi. It's Tommi. If you need something that can wait until I can call you back, leave a message. If it can't wait, call me downstairs. If I'm not there, call my cell."

Apparently, she assumed anyone calling would know "downstairs" was the bistro. Just as apparently, the majority of her callers had her various numbers.

The usual beep sounded.

"Tommi, it's Max," he said, resuming his pacing. "Call me when you get this. I'm at my condo. Here," he added, because he had one in Chicago, too, and started to leave his number when the line clicked again.

"Max? Wait. Let me turn this off." Her disembodied voice sounded faintly breathless. "There," she said, her voice clearer. "Sorry. I was down the hall."

"Are you okay?"

"I'm fine," Tommi replied, heading back across her small living room to close her door. Ignoring the effect of his voice on her heart rate, she flipped the latch and turned down the already low volume on the radio. "I was just down the hall helping Syd when I heard the phone."

"Why did Syd need help?"

"He used the wrong remote to change channels again. He'd picked up the one for the DVD, so he messed up his TV when he started punching buttons. He couldn't get his news show." Wearing sweats, she padded past her sage-colored sofa with its taupe throw pillows and botanical prints above it and sank into her favorite chair.

"If you're calling about the agreement, I'm almost finished reading it. That's what I was doing when Essie called." The document sat with her cup of now cool herbal tea and box of Puff Pops on the end table beside her. "It arrived Friday, but this morning was the first chance I've had to get to it. It was second on my list for today."

Curiosity entered his tone. "What was the first?"

"Sleeping in." The next item on her list was Christmas shopping for her staff and her family—which had provided the perfect excuse for not joining her mother for lunch. She needed pants, too. She hadn't been able to zip her jeans at all that morning.

"That would be a priority," he agreed, his deep voice shaded by something she couldn't quite identify. "How did your private parties go? Did you call the culinary school for backup?"

His casual questions came as a relief to her. It had been a week since she'd seen him, and their conversation that next day had been businesslike and brief. She just hadn't been able to forget how remote he'd seemed when he'd last walked out of her kitchen—or to escape the little ache that had grown the more she'd thought about what he'd lost so long ago. First, his mom. Then, the wife he'd hoped would anchor him after that loss.

She now knew he'd once wanted the ties that made a person feel committed, connected and a part of something more than himself. That desire clearly no longer existed. He'd somehow abandoned it—along with whatever dreams he'd once had of a family of his own.

Yet, he'd awakened those dreams in her.

She'd gone twenty-eight years without wanting to risk her heart and soul on a man. But she now knew what it was like to long for someone she could honestly share with, someone she could truly trust, someone she could love and who could love her back.

"I did," she told him, finding it truly ironic that the only man who'd ever managed that feat should be one with arrow-proof walls around his heart. "I had two students do prep work for me. Andrew and Shelby were totally on top of everything else."

"Maybe you should keep those students through the

holidays," he suggested. "Or go ahead and hire more help now if those students can't work when you need them."

"I won't need more permanent help until after the expansion."

"Has your energy come back?"

She'd turned sideways in the chair. With one leg drawn up, she blinked at the tiny hole in the knee of her sweats. "Pardon?"

"You said your energy was supposed to be coming back soon," he reminded her. "Has it?"

Concern. That was the note she hadn't been able to identify. It was also what had the tension easing from her shoulders.

"I think so." The effect of his voice was nice, almost as soothing as the strange calm his physical touch could bring. "It was a really busy week and I kept up, so it must be improving."

"How about the dizziness? Have you taken any more dives for the floor?"

"I never actually hit the floor," she reminded him.

"Only because I caught you."

"True," she conceded, remembering too easily how she'd found herself cradled against his rock-hard chest. Despite being so tired she could barely move, she'd fallen asleep with that memory last night. And the night before. And the night before that.

She really missed him.

"No more dives." She saw no harm in her silent admissions, or in indulging her little fantasy, or imagining the sense of protection she'd felt with him holding her. It wasn't like he'd ever know. "No more dizziness." The morning sickness had also ebbed considerably, but he hadn't known about that. The only reason she'd reached for the cereal this morning was because she'd craved it. That and green olives.

"Thanks for asking." Her hand unconsciously stole over her stomach. "It feels strange to answer questions like that."

"You still haven't told anyone else?"

"Not yet."

The sound of a television on his end had grown fainter. Moments ago, the volume had increased, only to ebb and rise again. She had the feeling he was pacing when his voice cut back in.

"Just so you know, I told Scott."

Caution had entered his tone, or maybe it was defense.

"I imagine you had to," she conceded. "Health and physical ability are legitimate considerations in a partnership. I've just been waiting to mention it to anyone else until our agreement is signed. I want to be able to honestly say my financial situation is secure. That will be important to my family.

"Especially my mom," she confided. "She's always been adamant about her girls being financially independent. I need her and my sisters to know I have everything under control."

With her legs tucked beneath her, she reached for her tea. Once the papers beside her were signed by her and L&C, she had no excuse to avoid her inevitable familial powwow. She would tell them all together. No way did she want to deal with repeat performances.

Her news would just be so much easier to deliver with Max there to support her. If nothing else, he'd distract the daylights out of her mom and the rest of the Fairchild women.

"Wouldn't all this have been easier if you'd just gone to Harry Hunt?"

She had her cup halfway to her mouth. At her Uncle Harry's name, her hand froze midair.

"I understand the need to be independent," Max insisted. "I just can't help wondering why you put yourself through hoops applying for loans and working out a partnership deal instead of going to him. It seems to me you could have saved yourself a whole lot of stress."

"How do you know I know him?"

"Scott said he introduced the two of you at some charity thing a while back. Hunt referred to you as his surrogate niece, and told him you're on his board of directors. I can't imagine why you'd need us with his kind of money. Or with what you must earn being on that board. Why didn't you list that as an asset? Or him as a reference?"

Uneasy, she drew back from setting the tea on the table.

"I don't earn anything from that position," she admitted, hopefully killing his assumptions about whatever wealth he thought came with the "perk" that felt more like an obligation than anything else. "Please tell me this isn't going to affect our partnership."

"This conversation has nothing to do with our agreement, Tommi. Other than that I don't understand why you want it.

"Now," he continued quietly, "what do you mean you don't earn anything from your position?"

Tommi rarely mentioned the Hunts to people who didn't already know their connection. She especially didn't mention to strangers why her family was connected to them to begin with.

But Max wasn't a stranger. He knew as much about her as anyone ever had.

The realization should have disturbed her. The only reason it didn't was because he'd exposed a part of himself to her she felt certain not many people knew about, either.

"My sisters are also all on the board. And my mom." All anyone had to do was look at the annual report to discover that. "Except for my mom's, all our positions are honorary. Uncle Harry gave them to us when we graduated from high school. He also gave each of us a monetary gift," she decided to call the $100,000 he'd bestowed on each of them. "That's how we paid for our educations, and how I opened the bistro. He's been generous to our family, but just because we know him doesn't mean we look at him or any of the Hunts as an ATM. We make our own way."

Any of the Hunts, she'd said.

J.T. would know her, Max thought.

"Mind telling me how you know them?"

"That would depend on why you're asking."

There was no mistaking her caution. Considering the wealth Harry Hunt and his sons possessed, he couldn't blame her. He didn't doubt for a moment that there were those who might try to get close to her just because of whatever influence she might have with any one of them.

His partner included.

He just wished that caution wasn't there. Not with him.

"I'm just asking…" As a friend, he thought, because that was the easiest way to excuse the protectiveness he felt toward her. "Because I'm trying to figure out the 'surrogate' part in all of this. I don't have any ulterior motives, Tommi." He set his mug of coffee on the slab of colored concrete his decorator had chosen as a coffee table. "If you'd rather I let it go, I will."

He didn't want to. But he would. For now.

For long moments, he heard nothing but the low drone of a pregame show on the flat-screen television above the granite fireplace. Behind the glass fireplace screen, flames shot in little jets from a bed of blue glass beads. He'd flipped on the gas switch as much to put some animation in the room as to take the edge off the chill. That was why he kept the TV on when he was there, too. All the hard, sleek surfaces in the high and expansive place looked great. They just didn't offer much in the way of warmth.

Odd, he thought, that he hadn't considered that until now.

"We know them because my father was Uncle Harry's business partner," he finally heard her say. "His sons are like cousins. They're older than we are, so we weren't close growing up, but they're like family."

"Your dad was his business partner?"

"Mom and my dad knew him even before they were married. I'm sure that's why Uncle Harry wanted to help with expenses after Dad died. And why he gave us the board positions later. They'd all known each other since they were kids."

"But your dad had to be worth plenty in his own right."

"He probably was," she quietly concluded. "I won't go into what all happened, and there's a lot I don't know, but he'd pretty much mismanaged his and mom's finances. We had to move and things changed quite a bit," she admitted, sparing him the details, "but we never went without anything we really needed. Mom insisted on that. She also insisted on taking care of everything herself. Uncle Harry got around that by focusing on us. Monetarily, anyway."

The man had never been much on personal connections, she told him. But her mom firmly believed education was the only road to true independence. Since that became the focus for all of her daughters, she allowed herself to accept whatever might enhance or fund that goal from Harry. But that was all.

Max listened for nuances, but Tommi never ventured near whatever it was her father had done to mismanage what must have been considerable assets. Even all those years ago, HuntCom would have been worth millions. Because he sensed she was protecting her father's memory and, maybe her mother, he wouldn't ask. Nor did he ask why she thought Harry wanted her married badly enough to offer a bribe to get the deed done. He didn't want anything to change the soft, confiding tones of her voice as he sat back on his leather sofa in his sweats and nursed the coffee that didn't taste anywhere near as good as hers did.

All he cared about just then was that she hadn't any more dizzy spells. Still hearing fatigue in her voice, it relieved him, too, to know she'd had a little extra help that week and that for the moment at least, she wasn't in her bistro, taking care of a dozen things at once.

As he admitted to her that he could now see why she hadn't gone to her surrogate uncle and they moved on to talk about when she might tell her family about her baby, he felt relieved, too, by the easy way she'd accepted his having told his partner about her circumstances.

He'd been struck before by her undemanding sense of forgiveness, her understanding. Not caring to examine why he was so drawn by that, he concentrated on what she said about finding the right time to break her news.

He suggested she do it right after she got her copy of the countersigned agreement back. Then, in a few days, it would be over with.

"Just tell them. You'll feel better," he insisted. "It'll be like dropping a hundred-pound weight."

He expected her hesitation. He just hadn't fully antici-pated its cause.

"I doubt I could get them all together this week," she finally prefaced, not sounding totally convinced of his logic anyway. "But about the agreement. There's something you need to know." The ease left her voice. "The monthly reports I'll send to your accounting department aren't going to show quite what you expect.

"I agreed to sign with the wage and benefit restrictions. And I will. I'm just not going to cut anyone's pay or benefits. It won't affect your investors' profit margin at all," she assured him in a rush. "I promise. I'll just make up the difference out of the increase you show I'll have in my salary. I just wanted you to know that because whoever gets that first report will probably freak when they see my payroll."

He could practically see her holding her breath. His own came out in a heavy sigh.

What she intended to do totally defeated part of what he wanted for her. At the very least, she wouldn't be able to afford her bigger apartment.

"Max?" she asked.

Rising, he drew his hand down his face.

"Really," she insisted, at his silence. "It won't affect anything. I'll just deposit part of my salary back into the partnership account. It's all just a matter of bookkeeping."

It affects you, he wanted to say. "You're right," he muttered, instead. "It won't affect their profits. Look. Don't mail the agreement. Are you going to be home today?"

"I need to leave in a while. But I should be back by six." She hesitated. "Why?"

"I'll come by after that and pick it up. I leave for Chicago in the morning, but I'll sign it and leave it with legal before I go."

She seemed relieved. Or maybe the relief was there because he hadn't questioned her totally unacceptable plan to take care of her employees.

She was good at that. Taking care of people.

She'd paused again, her silence making him think she had more to say. Apparently deciding not to push her luck, she opted to tell him she'd see him later, then, and left him staring at the phone in his hand.

The longer he sat there, the more he disliked what she intended to do. And the more convinced he became that it was time she let someone do something for her for a change.

He didn't bother to wonder why he wanted to be that someone. As he finally tossed the phone aside, all that mattered was that he knew exactly what that something should be.

Chapter Eight

It had seemed to Tommi as if all of Seattle had jammed itself into the wreath-and-garland-draped Pacific Place mall. She hadn't had much choice other than to brave the masses, though. Not with only one other full day off before Christmas.

Even with the sheer number of bodies reducing the odds of seeing anyone she knew, she'd been on her way to Barney's when she'd seen her mom and Georgie a level down across the wide atrium.

She regarded it a fair indication of how messed up her life had become that she promptly ducked her head and hurried on.

Since her cell phone hadn't chimed, they hadn't seen her. Still, guilt continued to nag at her for the way she'd been avoiding her family in general when she finally headed up the four flights of stairs from the garage to her third-floor apartment with her six shopping bags, her purse and a two-foot-high fiber-optic Christmas tree. *Faux* was as good as it was going to get this year.

She'd wanted to be out of the miserable cold and sheeting rain and home before six. Since she had only a few minutes before Max would be downstairs buzzing her apartment to let him in, she hurried as best she could. Until a couple of months ago, she could jog up all four flights and her lungs would barely notice it. Anymore, even without the packages, she tended to be out of breath by the time she reached the second floor.

She didn't even want to think about what the trek would feel like in five months. Or how she was going to handle the increased management responsibilities of an expansion and training more staff and being a new mom. What she did want was to crawl into bed, pull the blankets over her head and not wake up until summer. Then, when she did wake up, she wanted to find out that everything she'd been dealing with the past few months had just been a bad dream.

Readjusting the bag holding six tall rolls of Christmas wrap, she turned into the hall leading to her apartment.

Max was already there.

He leaned against the wall by her door, his squall jacket tossed over one shoulder of his heavy pullover, hands on the hips of his cargo pants.

Before she could do much more than hesitate at the unfamiliar reserve carved in his face, he unfolded his long frame and started toward her.

His glance swept hers, his brow pinching as he took the tree.

"How did you get in?" she asked, still clutching the only bag that wasn't looped over an arm.

"Essie buzzed me up."

She tried to look at her watch. Between her heavy coat

sleeve and the bag handles holding the fabric down, she couldn't see it. "I didn't think I was late."

"You're not. Give me those."

He closed in on her again, six feet of commanding masculinity that smelled of expensive aftershave and the butter mints Essie kept on her coffee table. As she gratefully turned over the heaviest of the bags, what she noticed most were the deepening lines in his forehead.

"What's in here?" he asked, still at her shoulder as she stuck her key into her door lock.

"Books."

"Like what," he muttered. "A set of encyclopedia?"

She felt guilty about her family, more overwhelmed than she dare admit by the changes taking place in her life and aware of him in ways she thought best not to consider, considering how badly she needed the calm in his touch. Still, she managed a smile.

"Close. I bought a vampire series for Bobbie's fiancé's daughter and a six-volume history of martial arts for his son." Keys rattled as she moved from upper lock to lower. "And a coffee-table book for Mom."

"Why didn't you leave all this in your car and let me bring it up? You knew I was coming."

She had the door open. With him behind her, she couldn't see his frown, but she could hear it in his voice. It was that unmistakable displeasure with her that had her regarding him a little skeptically when she stepped aside for him to enter.

Rather than tell him it hadn't occurred to her to impose on him, she let the admonishment go and motioned into her living room.

"Just put them anywhere."

Conscious of her caution, Max headed past a pillow-strewn sofa and the coffee table holding side-by-side copies of the agreement she'd been sent. The modest space wasn't at all what he'd expected. Still, it suited her just the same. The colors in her bistro were bright, edgy, bold. What she surrounded herself with in her home gave the impression of nature having come indoors. Everything was shades of green, pale cream, taupe or rich espresso. A tall, slender wood vase held long reeds by the cubes forming her entertainment center. The clean lines of her furnishings were covered in fabrics that invited touch.

There was calmness here. Comfort.

He heard the door close. By the time he had the little tree sitting on an end table and the bags in one of the two comfortable-looking barrel chairs flanking it, she'd come up beside him.

He hadn't seen her with her hair down before. That straight dark silk framed the gentle lines of her face, reflected touches of gold in the light from the overhead she'd flipped on. But something more had caught his attention.

He'd seen her looking a little tired before, but he'd never seen the sheer weariness that lurked just beneath her faint smile. He knew she'd had a long week, though. She'd also just spent the one day she could have been off her feet hiking through department, book and, from the logo on one of the bags, cooking stores.

"How long did all this shopping take you?"

"About six hours," she said, piling her remaining packages and her purse in the other chair. "All I have to do now is finish up the last of my list, wrap everything, and I'll be done."

She made it sound as if those tasks would take no time at all. Watching her slip off her coat and head for the closet by the door, he couldn't help but wonder if it was herself she was trying to convince of that. Or him.

"The agreement is right there," she said, nodding to the

copies on the table. "When you said you'd come get it and sign it here, I thought I'd wait to sign it, too."

He knew how important—and difficult—this partnership was for her. Had the deal been larger for L&C, the principals would have executed the paperwork together in a conference room or an office. Being large for her, it made sense that she'd want to acknowledge that significance by signing at the same time.

"May I take your jacket?"

"No need. I won't be here long. And you don't need to sign that agreement. Just give it to me."

He had his jacket tucked under his arm. Aware of how still she'd gone, he pulled a legal-sized envelope from a net inner pocket and laid the heavy garment atop the bags. He really didn't plan to stay. According to Syd, Sunday night was when Tommi did her books if she hadn't had time to do them during the week. Since he knew her week had been even busier than he'd suspected, thanks to the chatty neighbors who'd also told him about the two hundred Santa cupcakes she'd baked and decorated for Alaina's daughters' school's holiday bake sale, he was sure she'd be up with those books tonight.

She'd brought them up from her minuscule office downstairs. He could see them through the archway on her small kitchen table.

Confusion vied with disquiet in her deep brown eyes. "Why don't I need to sign it?"

"Because I think you'll like these terms better."

Seeing the familiar formatting on the two copies of the document he handed her, Tommi's glance darted to his, then back to the pages.

The heading was the same as the agreement she had left on the coffee table with her best pen. Only this one contained half as many pages, and it wasn't with Layman

& Callahan. It was with *Maxwell Alexander Callahan, an individual.*

Her confusion remained. "What's going on?"

Max wished he knew. He'd been going with his gut ever since he'd hung up with her that morning, and his gut was leading him into totally uncharted territory.

All he knew for certain was that he didn't want her mixed up in any way with his partner.

"My personal conditions aren't as strict as the company's. That agreement," he said, nodding to what she held, "doesn't restrict wages or benefits for your employees. My percentage is less, so you'll be able to cover the expense without going into your salary. The renovation clauses have changed, too.

"You'll still have to expand to earn enough to pay for your additional chef. There's no way around that." She already knew she couldn't afford the trained help she badly needed without a means to make more income. "But you'll be working with one of the architects from J. T. Hunt's firm out of Portland. I talked to him this morning. He said he thought you'd like Jessica Kaczynski, so she'll contact you after the first of the year.

"The dates and franchise clauses are all the same. The only other change was to delete all references to the company and change the reporting procedure," he continued. "You'll be sending your reports to my personal accountant. The rest of the legalese is the same."

"You know J.T.?"

"I have for years. We worked together when he was with HuntCom. When a client doesn't already have their own architect for an expansion, he's my first go-to."

With everything else he'd said, Tommi wasn't sure why his mention of Harry's second son had caught her so off guard. She'd known HuntCom was Max's client. But mention of her surrogate cousin was only a small part of what had her feeling totally thrown.

The onerous wage clause was gone. He had cut his own percentage to help her employees.

She wouldn't have to work with his partner.

Disbelief had her slowly shaking her head. "Why did you do this?"

Max searched the fragile lines of her face. The strain was still there, shadowing her eyes, making it clear she couldn't believe what she was hearing. Or more likely, he figured, unable to imagine why he would make such changes for her.

"I did it because I know how insecure you felt being raised without your dad. And because I know you feel bad about bringing up your child that way. There's nothing I can do about it not having a father, but I can give you a little extra financial security. With this agreement, you won't have to use your money to make up the difference in your employees' wages and benefits. You can use it to take care of yourself and your baby.

"That should help with your mother, too," he concluded, recalling that her concern there had also figured into what he'd done. "You said you need to be able to tell her you're financially secure. Now that you have the means for that security, you can."

Tommi stared at the document. She knew what she'd heard. She just couldn't see much of anything at the moment because his intention to ease part of what was always on her mind had tears threatening. Those tears blurred the print on the page.

Tears were so not like her. At least, they hadn't been before she'd gotten pregnant.

Stunned by how quickly the moisture had pooled, afraid he would see, she sank to the sofa. Head down, the pages in her lap, she drew a deep breath and blinked hard to bring the top page into focus.

All Max could see was the top of her head as she pulled her long, shining hair to one side, leaving it to fall straight as an arrow over the two-inch threads of liquid silver hanging from her ear.

It also covered the delicate curve of her cheek and the little dimple he knew would be there if she smiled.

The earrings had caught his attention out in the hall. The dimple he'd noticed the first time her soft-looking mouth had curved.

He wasn't sure when he'd first noticed the inherent grace about her as his glance moved over the long black tunic sweater covering her narrow shoulders and her slim black pants. Or when he'd first recognized her awareness of him in the way she seemed to breathe in a little before she would quickly look from his face. He'd done his best to detach himself from his attraction to her from the moment they'd met.

Because she needed far more than he was capable of giving her, he tried to detach himself now.

"Unless you want to reread all of it," he said, not totally sure what she thought of what he'd done, "the main changes are on the first three pages and the last one."

He turned away, listened to the sound of the pages turning. He didn't think she'd have a problem with his arbitrary alterations. Not as troubled as she'd been by the other terms. He just hoped she trusted him enough to accept what he'd offered.

That he wanted her to trust him—him, not his company—was something he hadn't realized until she picked up the pen from above the old agreement.

Apparently okay with the changes, she signed her name on the last page. Picking up the other copy, she did the same.

"Your turn," she murmured, still not looking up.

Max stepped between the sofa and coffee table. Her eyes still stinging, the moment he did, Tommi rose, quickly turning away to slip around the opposite end so he could sit where she had.

With her back to him, facing her purchases, she drew a long, quiet breath. She could hear the faint scrape of pen on paper as he slashed his signature next to hers on both copies. Then, the rustle of papers as he stuffed the old agreement and his own copy of the new one into the manila envelope.

She rubbed her breastbone. Gratitude was there, huge and squeezing hard at her heart. So was the need to let him know that.

So was the need to be more like him.

He didn't seem to require anything from anyone. Least of all her. He'd made that clear enough the last time he'd walked out of her kitchen. Hating how needy she felt herself just then, she would have given anything to possess his self-contained defenses. It was his fault she felt this way, after all. She'd always stood on her own. She'd been raised to do exactly that. It hadn't been until he'd come along that she'd become so acutely aware of how very tired she was pretending to be strong all by herself.

Her throat burned.

Over the heavy beat of rain on her windows, she heard Max bump the coffee table and the rustling of his movements at the other chair as he put the manila envelope inside his jacket. Coming up beside her, he held out her copy of what had now been signed, dated and, literally, delivered.

With her head still down as if she was looking at the agreement, she took it along with another determined breath and blinked. Hard. But instead of clearing her vision, all she succeeded in doing was squeezing out one of the tears she'd tried to hold back.

That single drop landed near the bottom of the page.

The soft plop was met with Max's quiet, "Hey."

Forcing a little laugh, she looked up.

"Ignore me," she insisted, wiping at another tear trailing down her cheek. "This is just hormones." And fatigue. But she didn't dare think about how tired she really was. Tired of uncertainty, of guilt, of worry. If she did, she wouldn't stop crying until morning. "They've been messing with me for months."

She tried to smile. With the embarrassing tears still coming, she ducked her head again. "Thank you, Max. You have no idea how much I appreciate this." She sniffed. Tried to laugh. "I can obviously handle you better when you're being impossible."

He hadn't been sure how she'd react to what he'd done. What he definitely hadn't expected were the tears that had him feeling a little unnerved. They weren't angry or accusatory. She wasn't using them to make him feel bad, or get her way or otherwise maneuver or manipulate. Those he could have handled. He'd become immune to that sort of weeping along about the time he'd realized some women could turn the waterworks on and off at will. But hers were there because he had helped her.

"And I can handle you better when you don't look the way you do right now.

"Don't," he insisted, catching her by the shoulders when she started to turn away.

She'd misunderstood. There had been times when she'd looked seriously in need of being held. With her unguarded brown eyes glistening with unshed tears, her dark lashes spiky from those that had escaped, she'd never looked more in need of that than she did now.

"I didn't mean that in a bad way." Conscious of how easily she seemed to accept his touch, wondering if she had any idea how that affected a man, he left his hands to rest where they were. What he'd meant was that there were times when she could make him forget he should only be thinking about business with her.

Like now. Now, all he wanted was for the tears he'd so inadvertently caused to go away.

For a moment, he wasn't at all sure what he should do. Since he was going on his gut with her, he decided that was all he could do now.

"Come here," he murmured.

Beneath his hands, he felt her shoulders rise with the shuddery breath she drew. That was her only hesitation before she moved into his arms. As trusting as a child, she curled her fists between them and rested her forehead against his chest.

He heard her breath shudder out, felt her sink closer.

"Will you tell me something?" she asked, her throat sounding tight.

The feel of her curvy little body leaning into his had his own voice going a little rough. "Sure."

"How do you not get tired of handling your life on your own? I'm usually pretty good at it," she said, a catch in her muffled tones. "But I could use some hints."

Rain beat on the windows behind the drawn drapes. The only other sound in the room was of the wind driving the rain in sheets.

"I've never thought about it."

Her shaky voice went quieter. "Well, when you do, will you let me know? I think I want to be more like you."

Her conclusion disturbed him. He just didn't bother to go below the surface of what she'd wanted him to reveal.

His only thought was that the last thing she needed was him for a role model.

"You're just tired," he said. "You need to rest."

"I can't rest. I need to do my books."

He cupped his hand over the back of her head, then skimmed it down the dark length of her hair with a quiet "Shh."

He did it once more, slowly, letting his fingers drift to where its softness ended between her shoulder blades before starting all over again. As he did, he couldn't help notice how delicate the bones of her spine felt, how small and fragile she really was.

Small and fragile and badly in need of feeling in control.

He knew how important control was to her. As important as it was to him, the need had been easy to recognize. What didn't seem so familiar were the responses she stirred as he breathed in the fresh scent of her hair and let the long strands slide beneath his fingers.

Her physical effect on him he didn't question. He couldn't be in the same room with her without wanting to touch her the way he was now. Without wanting far more. She'd invaded his mind and his sleep and the concern he felt for her had him acting without question. With her body so close, still wondering at how instinctively she'd come to him, there wasn't a fiber of his being that wasn't aware of her effect on him now. It was how she made him feel deeper inside that felt so alien.

It was good to know he could make the partnership a little easier on her, and give her more peace of mind about her situation. After all, making sure she could take care of her bistro and her baby was what she'd been after all along. In the back of his mind lurked the knowledge that Scott might fight him over what he'd done with the agreement, out of ego and annoyance more than anything else. But the thought disappeared as he listened to her shuddery breaths and tried to ignore the effect of her scent and her softness on certain parts of his body.

Feeling good about something he'd done seemed rarer all the time. And what he'd done felt right.

So did holding her.

He'd never offered comfort to a woman before. He wasn't at all sure how a man went about it. But his unpracticed motions seemed to soothe her, so he continued until her deep breaths gave way to a stillness that had him nudging up her chin to see how she was doing.

She lifted her hands from his chest. Refusing to look up, she swiped at her cheek.

"I'm sorry, Max."

Slipping his fingers beneath her jaw, he tipped her face to his.

Silent tears glistened in her eyes, continued to streak toward her chin.

He caught one with his thumb, drew it toward the lush fullness of her lower lip. Another slid into its place.

Without thinking, he cradled her face between his hands, and caught it with his lips at the corner of her mouth. She'd looked as helpless as she'd sounded.

"Stop," he begged, the salt of her tears mingling with the sweetness of her skin.

Her breath trembled out. "I'm trying."

Brushing his lips across hers, he caught a tear on the other side.

"Try harder."

His gentle command vibrated against her mouth. He held her with such tenderness, as if she were something delicate, breakable. That was how Tommi felt as he kissed away what felt like months of stress.

The calm she'd craved in his touch had come the moment he'd pulled her into his arms. In the space of a sigh, she'd felt the tension drain from her muscles like air from a falling soufflé. Yet, that relieving calm hadn't stopped the tears. It had just allowed them to flow more freely. Much like the almost unbearable gentleness of his lips when his mouth settled over hers and he eased her back against his big body.

He tasted of warmth and butter mint as he opened her to him, touched his tongue to hers. That warmth stole through her, melting her, testing the steadiness of her legs. Beneath her hand she felt the hard beat of his heart.

This was exactly where she wanted to be. Where she needed to be. With him holding her, kissing her, she could almost feel the insecurities plaguing her lessen their relentless grasp.

The gratitude she'd felt before compounded itself. He was doing the very thing she needed the most just then. He was letting her lean on him while he helped her cope with the tears that would have felt so awful had she been dealing with them alone. He was taking care of her. He'd done that in little ways before. It was what he'd been doing when he'd said he wanted to give her a little more security. She could only imagine how little of that he'd had in his own life from the moment of his birth—until he'd created that security for himself.

It was that kind of strength she sought from him as he robbed what little stability remained in her knees and she locked her hands around his neck to stay upright. She needed so badly what she felt in him; what she felt with him.

Stretched the length of his long, hard body, she heard him groan. Or maybe the small moan had been hers.

Max swallowed that achy little sound as he slipped his

hand behind her head, drinking more deeply of the sweet, intoxicating taste of her.

He'd felt her against him before, but not like this. Not with every inch of her seeking every inch of him. The impressions that had remained after he'd caught her to his chest when she'd fainted had been burned into his brain. Too easily he'd been taunted by the memory of the enticing curve of her hip, the tempting fullness of her breasts. Too often he'd found himself pumping a little more iron or running an extra mile to exhaust the physical ache the memory would bring.

That ache was there now as he shaped that curve and absorbed the sensual feel of that fullness straining against him. With her mouth so soft and willing beneath his, her body fitted so perfectly to him, he drew his hand down the long line of her back, pressed in at the base of her spine.

He hissed in a breath. At the feel of her against his arousal, he went still. He thought for sure she would pull back, create a little distance from what threatened to become something more than she was looking for. He had the feeling she was searching for comfort more than anything physical. But there could be no doubt in her mind that he wanted her. Letting her go would be easier than denying himself oxygen. He would, though. If that was what she wanted.

She'd gone a little still herself. Yet, within a heartbeat, he felt her arms tighten around him and their lips met again.

She was like a drug in his blood. The very essence of her seemed to steal through his veins, threatening to destroy reason, demanding more.

That demand increased by slow degrees.

He definitely wanted her. He wanted the feel of her. All of her.

Her bedroom was right behind him. He'd noticed it through its open door in a small hall when he walked in.

He was no saint. While he cared about her in ways he had no intention of exploring, he could only deny himself so much. With his heart hammering, he slipped his hands up her arms. Circling her wrists, he drew her hands to his chest.

"I can't do this," he said, his voice a low rasp. He needed distraction. He needed to let her go. "Your books." He released one of her hands, skimmed his fingers over the curve of her tear-stained cheek. "You said you needed to do them. I'll help."

Confusion swept her face. He could feel the faint trembling of her pulse with this thumbs as she looked up at him, her eyes luminous, her lips swollen and damp from her tears and his kisses.

"My books?"

"If we don't do something else, I'm going to kiss you again. If I do that," he warned her, "I won't want to stop there."

He was giving her fair notice. Yet, she remained motionless, looking totally susceptible to him in the moments before she drew another ragged breath.

"I don't want to do them now."

With the back of his knuckles, he traced the delicate line of her jaw. He'd never seen her look so vulnerable.

"Then, what do you want?"

"I don't want to have to think."

"What do you mean?"

She swallowed at his touch. "I just want…"

"What?" he prodded, when her voice trailed off.

"What you make me feel."

Moments ago, he'd thought she was only looking for

comfort. At her quiet admission, he realized now that she might well be looking for escape.

It occurred to him vaguely that there was something dangerous about going on nothing but instinct with her. Already craving her, drawn by the silent plea in her eyes, he just couldn't remember what that something was.

Curving his fingers around the back of her neck, he tipped her mouth to his.

"I can arrange that."

"Please."

He had barely lowered his head to capture her faint appeal when Tommi slipped her arms back around his neck.

She didn't think she'd have been able to bear it if he'd let her go. Not when, for the first time in months, she was only thinking of the moment. And not when she'd just realized it was more than his strength that she needed, and infinitely far more than gratitude that she felt.

She was falling in love with him. She knew that to the very core of her being. The realization should have stunned her, she supposed, as his hands slowly worked beneath her sweater. Instead, what settled over her in the long, debilitating moments before he turned her toward her bedroom was unquestioning acceptance. Loving him seemed as if it was simply supposed to be.

She'd told him she just wanted what he made her feel. She just hadn't realized how much more there could be as their mouths mated and he backed her through the doorway. His hands were on the bare skin of her waist, greedy for the feel of her. Hers slid under the shirt beneath his pullover, just wanting to be closer.

The first time he'd touched her, she'd experienced something with him she'd never felt with anyone before. But what she'd thought of as his calming effect on her, she now realized had been an instinctive sort of trust. It was as if, at that very moment, she had known she would be safe with him.

That must have been the moment he had claimed her heart.

Claiming her was what he seemed to be doing now as he pulled off her sweater, withdrawing his touch only long enough to grip the back of his own and pull it over his head. The chill in the dim and cozy room barely registered before he drew her against the corrugated muscles of his abdomen and his hard, honed chest. His heat flowed into her, warming her skin and her blood while he unfastened her bra and tumbled them onto her unmade bed with his mouth seeking hers.

She sought him back, her hands slipping over the roping muscles of his biceps and shoulders. He was beautiful to her, strong, so powerfully male. All that latent power made his restraint and his gentleness so much more overwhelming when he eased back to trail a path of slow burning fire down the side of her neck to the fullness of her exquisitely sensitive breasts.

She'd never known what it was to be touched so tenderly, or to need so badly to touch back as he encouraged her to caress and he caressed. To explore. Or simply to cling to him if that was what she wanted.

That was what she wanted most; the feel of his arms around her. Yet, after he enlisted her help stripping away the rest of their clothes and his hands started roaming over her body again, she wanted that, too.

He seemed to absorb her as he molded his hands to the shape of her ribs, her hips, the slight curve of her stomach.

"You're beautiful," he told her, whispering the words in her ear as he stroked her long limbs and sensitive places.

She touched him back, emboldened by the caresses that made her feel as if she was somehow necessary to him. As essential as he was becoming to her, the raw hunger she tasted in him became her own. She just wasn't at all certain what she felt when his fingers moved to splay again over the gentle curve of her belly and he lifted his head to look into her eyes.

With the room in shadows, she could see little in his taut and tortured features. He didn't allow her any time to search. He found her mouth again, pressing her to him with such possession that she forgot everything but the need to let him know with her body what was far too soon to express with words.

With his control paper-thin, the feel of her seeking him was pushing him precariously close to the edge. Their breaths mingled, every intake of his own bringing hers inside him to seep into his cells. What had begun as a need to comfort had long since given way to the demanding need to possess.

Even with that need driving him, the functioning part of Max's brain slowed him down long enough to reach for the protection he'd pulled from his wallet. He resented that barrier separating him from her, wasn't even sure why he was using it. But the finer points of Tommi already being pregnant and the need to protect her weren't anything he would debate. Not when he ached for her so badly he could barely breathe.

There was no denying his need. Or her own when she reached for him. Aligning her infinitely softer curves to his hard angles and planes, fighting the more urgent demands of his body, he eased himself into her. With her arching to him, her heat surrounding him, the edges of what control he had began to fray. But it was only after he heard her whisper his name and felt her shatter that he let go. The instant he did, his awareness narrowed to nothing but the woman punching holes in nearly every barrier he possessed, and the searing heat that evaporated conscious thought.

A shaft of pale light from the living room slanted near the foot of the bed, casting the room in shades of gray. The beat of rain against the window registered dimly in that cocooning twilight.

Tommi lay curled in his arms, her head tucked into his chest, her breathing slow and even. As Max turned his head toward the clock on her nightstand, he figured it was the storm that had wakened him.

The digits glowed 3:57 in neon green.

He hadn't intended to fall asleep. But then, he hadn't been prepared for the unfamiliar peace that had stolen over him after their breathing had quieted and they'd settled into each other's arms. That peace had lulled him with its strange contentment, luring him from any thought other than how good it was to simply hold her.

Peace was not what he felt now.

The realization that he'd complicated the hell out of their relationship had his mind up and fully functioning in the time it took him to swear at himself. So did the fact that he'd miss his flight if he didn't get himself out of there.

From the tension he could feel in Tommi's slender muscles, he knew she was now awake, too.

"Max?"

He'd told her yesterday morning he was going to Chicago. He just hadn't mentioned how early his flight was.

"We fell asleep," he whispered. He brushed her hair back from her shoulder, touching his lips to her temple to forestall the disquiet he already sensed in her. "I have to go." Easing his arm from under her, defenses already at battle with self-reproach, he turned away. "I'm late."

Bedding rustled as he swung his feet to the floor and snatched up his pants and briefs. When he'd shown up at her door last night, all he'd wanted was to make things a little easier for her. The last thing he wanted now was to bolt from her bed and leave her alone with whatever was going through her head.

Though he didn't have a lot of choice, it was probably better this way.

He swore again. He had two hours to get home, pack, run by the office and get to the airport. Less than that, actually. Early morning security could be a nightmare.

He had his pants zipped and was pulling his sweater over his head when he realized she was out of bed, too.

Her head popped through the neck of the sweater he had stripped from her last night. "What time does your plane leave?"

"Seven-ten. And I have to go by the office."

"Oh, Max. You'll barely make it."

"I'll do it somehow," he said, tying his boots. "Come to the door with me so you can lock it."

She'd barely pushed back her tangled hair and rounded the bed when he took her hand. The lights were still on in the living room. Tugging her with him, aware of her long bare legs, he led her to the chairs by the sofa and picked up his jacket from atop her packages. Noticing the manila envelope on the end table, he picked it up, too, and headed for the door.

She was right beside him.

"I'm sorry about this, Tommi." A muscle in his jaw jerked as he cupped one side of her face with his palm. Almost unconsciously, her head moved toward his touch.

Thoughts of how trustingly she'd stepped into his arms

flooded back. He was in uncharted waters with this woman, going with a current that threatened to become an undertow. Feeling distinctly threatened by that, he banished the memory as quickly as it had arisen.

Not totally sure what else he felt just then, certain only that guilt was involved, he closed his eyes on the uncertainty he could see in hers and brushed a kiss against her forehead.

"Make your call to your chef today. Then call me on my cell and let me know how the conversation went. If I don't answer, leave a message and I'll call you back."

"I will. And, Max," she said, curling her hand over his arm when he reached for the latch, "have a safe trip. Okay?"

He was anxious to go. Still, he hesitated long enough to murmur, "Sure," and give her a little half smile before he opened the door.

Seconds later, he was gone.

A minute after that, with the wall clock indicating that it was time to get up, Tommi was trying hard to believe his apology had only been for having bolted from her bed—and not for the regret she could have sworn she'd seen in his eyes before he'd turned away.

Chapter Nine

The uncertainties Tommi had managed to escape last night were back with a vengeance. Plus one.

She was in love with her business partner.

Her only defense for that disturbing circumstance was that she had no defenses at all where Max was concerned. She hadn't even tried to raise any. At least, none that had counted. She had somewhat feebly tried to dismiss her attraction to him as hormones run amok, but even when it had started becoming clear that he didn't want or need anything more than the life he already had, she hadn't tried to protect herself. Nowhere along the line could she think of a single thing she'd done to not fall in love with him.

The recriminations echoed in her head as she measured and scooped, stirred and chopped. Worse, no matter how hard she tried, she couldn't stop thinking about the way he'd looked when he'd left. It didn't help the uncertainty gripping her that he hadn't really kissed her before he'd gone. The brush of his lips on her forehead had felt horribly like a brush-off.

What did help was knowing that he wanted her to call after she'd talked to Kyle Madsen, the sous chef she so desperately wanted to hire. Thanks to her partnership with the man who'd thrown her already upended life a seriously disconcerting curve, she now had the means to do that.

Because she badly needed to focus on positives, as soon as the morning rush of regular customers who darted in for scones and lattes to go had eased, she was on the phone to the man she'd bonded with over béarnaise in sauce class. She and Kyle had hung out together so much in culinary school that people had assumed they were a couple, but he'd really been more like a brother to her. As for romance, it had been she who'd encouraged him to ask out the shy Tari Ling from breads and pastries. Six months later, she'd been Tari's maid of honor at their wedding.

Having worked through the details with Kyle, it was Tari she said goodbye to when she ended the call and walked out of her office to tell Alaina that she'd just hired a sous chef they were all going to love.

Since her staff had all endured her previous attempts to fill the position, her assurance had Alaina smiling—which temporarily took the woman's mind off the fact that her apparently opinionated and meddlesome mother had just announced her intention to come for Christmas.

Tommi knew that sort of dread. Her own mom wasn't what she'd call meddlesome, but she definitely had her opinions. Worse, she had a way of looking at Tommi that let her know without a single word that she'd disappointed her, let her down or otherwise not fulfilled her expectations.

Now that she had her business matters under control, she had few excuses to put off facing that disappointment. As Max had said, she'd feel better once she wasn't keeping her situation from her family. What he hadn't mentioned was the logistics of getting from Point A to Point B. But the man was a professional negotiator. When she walked into her office to call him right after Alaina left, she decided she'd ask if he thought she'd have a better advantage breaking her news on Christmas at her mom's, or if she should arrange to be on her own turf.

She was torn either way.

Torn was pretty much how she felt as she punched out his number and took a deep breath. She knew there was a two-hour time difference between Seattle and Chicago, but she had no idea what his schedule was. Since he'd said to leave a message if he didn't answer, that was what she would do.

He answered on the third ring.

"Tommi," he said, obviously having checked his caller ID. "Did you hire him?"

She wasn't sure which came as a greater relief. How quickly he'd answered or how normal his deep voice sounded to her.

Clutching the receiver a little more tightly, she sank to her desk chair. "He's starting in three weeks."

"Hey, that's great." The sounds of traffic filtered into her ear. The nearby honk of a horn, the distant sound of a siren. "I thought he wasn't available until February."

"He wasn't. But he and Tari are anxious to get up here. He said they'd make it work."

"I like his attitude. The sooner he starts, the better for you. It'll make the transition to twice as many customers after the expansion smoother, too. But you still need a relief cook."

She told him she realized that. She also mentioned that Kyle thought the expansion a great idea and that he'd be a huge help interviewing for extra staff. His wife was even interested in the position as part-time pastry chef.

"It's good to hear you talking bigger. And I'm glad you got him," he told her, sounding as rushed as the noisy traffic around him. "It has to feel good to get that out of the way.

"Listen," he continued, before she could say another word. "I'm going to have to go. I need to grab a cab." He paused, apparently distracted. "I'll try to call you later."

Disappointment made her hesitate. "Sure," she said, forcing that quick letdown from her voice. "No problem."

With a muffled "Okay, then," the connection went dead.

He was obviously in a hurry. Probably preoccupied, too, she thought, as her disappointment sank deeper. She'd wanted to tell him that it did feel good to have finally hired Kyle. And that she wasn't thinking bigger, so much as she'd just been acknowledging the next step she had to take. She needed to think about the expansion in terms of one thing at a time. If she looked too closely at the big picture, she'd feel overwhelmed all over again by what she'd agreed to do with a baby on the way. But he could have talked her through that. He was good at talking her through things.

She hadn't had a chance to ask how his meetings were going, either.

On the positive side, he hadn't said anything to make her think he felt the regret she'd sensed in him before he walked out her door. But then, he hadn't ventured anywhere near what had happened between them. He'd stuck strictly to business.

Taking her cue from him, she went back to work herself, trying hard not to dwell on how confused he had her. Yet, that confusion only increased when Essie and Syd showed up at four o'clock for their usual early dinner.

When the weather was as rainy as it was now, her elderly neighbors would forego the exercise of walking around to her back door and call down so she or whichever of her staff was there could let them in the front.

They arrived talking about what a nice visit they'd had with Max. It seemed he'd buzzed their apartment at five o'clock yesterday, told them he was to meet her at six, but wanted to know if he could see them first.

Remembering him from the day they'd met him in her kitchen, they'd let him in out of curiosity as much as anything else, Essie admitted. But their curiosity had turned to surprise when he'd given them a new remote control for their television, the universal kind they could use so Syd wouldn't keep using the wrong one to change channels and switching them to the DVD.

Since Syd could never figure out how to get back to where he wanted to be, Max had spent nearly an hour programming, writing down instructions and explaining how to use the device, and suggested they put the other controls away.

Syd claimed himself eternally beholden for the useful little gadget.

As for Essie, she declared Max sweet on Tommi since he'd kept checking his watch so he wouldn't be late, and "such a nice man" for asking Syd how his letter-writing campaign against the area's condo conversions was going.

He had made their day. Their week, actually. They were still talking about him when they came down the next afternoon.

What he had done for them had been very kind—and considerate and thoughtful. And so like him, Tommi realized, because she was learning that he showed he cared about people in unexpected ways. She would have told him that, too. The part about thinking him kind, considerate and thoughtful, anyway. But he hadn't called last evening as she'd hoped he would.

He didn't call that day, either.

Or the next.

Not daring to consider what his growing silence meant, Tommi made herself focus as best she could on preparations for the private dinner booked for the following evening. She wished it would stop raining so hard. As nasty as it was outside and with people occupied with shopping and other holiday demands and functions, the bistro had been unusually quiet that night. She needed to be busy. Busy was good. Busy meant she didn't have extra time to worry about why Max wasn't calling her back. But then, he hadn't said he would. He'd only said he'd "try."

As she dusted flour from her hands and told herself to stop obsessing, Shelby poked her head into the kitchen and told her a gentleman wanted to see her.

"He said his name is Scott Layman. Do you want to see him in here, or out front?"

Tommi's first response was a quick frown of incomprehension as she picked up a towel to wipe her hands.

"Out front is fine," she replied, unable to imagine what Scott was doing there. "Tell him I'll be right out."

With a quick nod and a "Will do," her waitress headed back into the bistro.

Walking up to the "out" door when it swung closed, Tommi peeked through its little window. Of the twelve customers she'd had that evening, only three remained. Of those, a gentleman who'd dined alone was thanking Shelby and preparing to leave. The couple at the corner table had just finished checking their bill and slid its folder to the edge of their table.

With a smile for the departing patron when she walked into the bistro herself, Tommi moved to the man at the wine bar.

Rainwater dripped from Scott Layman's red parka as he perused the specials on the chalkboard. He was an impressive man; tall, blond and built like a linebacker. As she'd remembered, he was also quick with a smile.

"Hey," he said, turning as she approached. Without a blink, his glance made an expert sweep from the cap covering her hair, over her now barely camouflaging chef's jacket and bounced back up. "It's good to see you again, Tommi."

"You, too," she replied, torn between ignoring the way he'd just checked her out and trying to imagine why he was there. "Are you here for dinner?"

"I already ate. I wish I hadn't now," he said, nodding toward the chalkboard propped at the end of the bar. "Beef bourguignonne is my all-time favorite." He glanced around the nearly empty establishment, smiled at Shelby as she walked past him with the couple's bill. "I'll have a glass of wine, though…if you have time to have one with me," he qualified. His smile broadened. "We can celebrate."

"Celebrate?"

"I brought our partnership agreement for the bistro." Looking as if he thought she'd be pleased, he opened the leather folder he'd set on the bar. Inside was a manila envelope that looked very much like the one Max had taken with him. "I was looking for something in Max's office a while ago and noticed that it wasn't signed yet. Sorry I haven't been around to get the deal sealed sooner, but we can get it done now."

A distinctly uncomfortable feeling gripped Tommi as Shelby darted a glance toward them. The girl's curiosity moved to quick concern as she ran the couple's credit card behind the bar. Concern and needless speculation were the very reasons Tommi hadn't wanted her staff to know she'd been looking to bring another party into the business until she could assure them that all would be well.

The man not only suffered a total lack of discretion, he apparently had no idea she wouldn't be working with him or his company. Max had obviously removed the agreement they'd signed from the envelope.

The professional in her refused to discuss business in front of customers or staff. Of equal concern was that Scott obviously felt he was doing the right thing by her.

"Why don't we go in the kitchen?"

"Whatever's best for you," he said, picking up the portfolio. "This is a really great place," he continued, enumerating what he saw as its charms as she led the way.

"I like the paintings out there. Good setup in here, too," he concluded, as she stopped in the alcove outside her office. "Max was right. You have a lot of potential here."

Considering his enthusiasm, she expected to find him looking around her tidy kitchen when she turned. Instead, he seemed far more interested in the double-breasted chef's coat running from her neck to just below her hips. Or, more specifically, imagining what she might look like without it.

Max had told him she was pregnant.

Knowing that the man eyeing her with such speculation possessed that knowledge made her decidedly uncomfortable.

With another dimension added to her unease, she scrambled for what she needed to say. "Thank you," she murmured, buying herself time. "I'm pretty partial to all of it myself."

She hated the position she found herself in. She hated even more that Max hadn't told Scott of the new arrangement himself. Or at least, mentioned to her that he hadn't yet discussed the change with his partner. But then, talk of the partnership a few nights ago had been totally forgotten along about the time he'd pulled her into his arms.

"So, you want to sign this and give me a tour?"

His tone was as affable as his expression. Her own manner remained considerably more subdued.

"I feel really awkward, Scott." She spoke the admission quietly, hoping her tone would encourage him to lower the heartier quality of his. "I'm not going into partnership with Layman & Callahan. I've signed a different agreement."

Genuine confusion lowered his wide brow. "What are you talking about?"

"Some of your company's terms were more restrictive than I was comfortable with. Max wouldn't modify them because of his obligations to your company's investors," she explained, certain this man would appreciate the protection of their clients' interests. "But he was kind enough to make those concessions as a private investor and offered to be my silent partner himself.

"Since he's out of town," she continued, picking her words carefully as she hurried to defend what Max had done, "he must not have had a chance to tell you about the change."

From the corner of her eye, she noticed the kitchen door swing in as Shelby entered with the water glasses she'd just cleared from the last customers' tables.

With a quick glance toward the office, Shelby caught the equally swift shake of her boss's head, the big, square-jawed man's fading good nature, and went right back out, leaving the door to swing closed.

The easy friendliness had left Scott's expression. As he pulled his BlackBerry from his belt clip and punched at its buttons, what Tommi saw now was an uneasy combination of baited embarrassment and displeasure.

Avoiding her eyes, he thumbed buttons to bring up whatever it was he was looking for. From the way his mouth pinched when he apparently found it, she had the feeling he'd noticed the message before. For whatever reason, he just hadn't chosen to open it until then.

Apparently, the post was brief.

With a poke at a button, Scott huffed a dismissing little, "Huh," and slipped the BlackBerry back onto its clip. "Guess I should have read my email. Max said we're not doing business with you. That he took care of it. My mistake."

"I'm sorry," she murmured, feeling bad for the big guy. "I really am, Scott. I think there's been more than a little miscommunication with all this. And not just with Max," she allowed. "None of it is your fault."

She was thinking of her Uncle Harry, and how he'd attempted to set the two of them up. She didn't know what Harry had said to him, but from the very first call Scott had made to her to apologize for leaving her waiting, it had been apparent that he had more than business on his mind. Since it had to be equally apparent from her failure to respond to his enticements that she'd never been interested in anything but business with him, she figured he could be feeling a little uncomfortable about that, too.

That discomfort, however, had already been masked.

"Hey, no problem. Misunderstandings happen." His smile returned. It held no humor, though. If anything, whatever he was thinking robbed the expression of anything resembling friendliness. "But just so you have the full picture yourself, I think you should know that Max wasn't just being 'kind' with his offer.

"Don't get me wrong," he insisted. "There's no one better

when it comes to getting the best deal for our company. Or for himself," he emphasized. "He's made us both rich doing just that. But he stands to gain far more from you than just having your little business in his personal portfolio. Has he already made his move on you?"

She didn't much care for the unpleasant edge in his tone. Or for the question. Considering that her fragile relationship with Max was none of this man's business, she refused to address it. "I don't understand," she admitted, referring to what else he'd said. "I don't have anything but this bistro—"

"You have a connection to Harry Hunt. And your Uncle Harry wants you married."

She blinked. In disbelief, she blinked again.

"He told you that?"

"He did. He said it was time you got married and gave your mother grandchildren...or something like that. I take it he either doesn't know you're already ahead of the game on that last part, or he's trying to help you out because you are."

Stunned, or maybe it was horrified, Tommi opened her mouth, closed it again.

Max's partner almost looked sympathetic. "That's why Harry wanted me to meet you a couple of weeks ago. Along with a few other perks, he offered me a seat on his board of directors if I got serious about you. I was planning to tell you that over dinner," he claimed, oblivious to how he'd just added insult to indignity. "I wanted you to know up front I wasn't interested in any of that. And to give you a heads-up about my partner."

He shook his head, his mouth pinching as if he felt he had no choice but to offer his warning. "It's pretty obvious from what Max has said about you and what he did with that agreement, that he's out to work his own deal with your uncle. You really should watch your back with him."

If he meant to sound concerned about her being taken advantage of, he didn't succeed. His tone was too self-serving to be mistaken for anything resembling the altruism he claimed. So was his vaguely satisfied look when he stepped back.

Pushing open the kitchen door, he looked toward the front windows with their trim of little white lights, then glanced back to where she remained a few feet away.

"It's still raining," he said, his tone affable once more. "Nothing like Seattle in December, is there?" He gave her a nod. "Have a good evening."

She caught the door as he let it go.

"You have a good one, too," she heard him say to Shelby.

Her waitress was resetting the tables the last of their customers had vacated. Looking a little uncertain, Shelby offered an accommodating "Good night," as he headed to the front door.

Tommi didn't say a word. She just stood there until he'd gone, then hurried between the tables to throw the locks and lower the Closed shade.

Her heart felt as if it were beating hard enough to bruise ribs. She didn't believe for an instant that Max would use her with her Uncle Harry. She knew he was ambitious. She knew he was driven, though she had no idea if he was pushing himself toward something or away from it. She wondered if he even knew. But Max had too many walls up for a man intent on charming his way into a woman's life. She'd seen a couple of cracks in those barriers, but she couldn't believe they were anywhere near coming down. It also seemed to her that a man intent on pursuing a relationship would have found time by now to let her know he was thinking about her.

When she turned back, Shelby's uncertainty had compounded itself.

"Is everything okay, Tommi?"

At the young woman's clear apprehension, Tommi drew a deep breath. This is so what she'd wanted to spare her help. "You mean with the bistro?" she asked, not totally sure what all she'd heard.

Behind her narrow, ebony-framed glasses, Shelby's kohl-rimmed eyes were as dark as her black uniform. They also looked huge. "That guy said he's going to be your partner?"

"What else did you hear?"

"Just something about Max making some concessions or something."

She apparently hadn't heard the part about Harry trying to marry her off. Grateful for that reprieve, she gave Shelby's arm a reassuring squeeze.

"First, everything is fine with the bistro," she promised, consciously omitting reference to the state of her personal life. "Your job is secure. So is everyone else's," she was quick to add. "We'll have a staff meeting tomorrow and I'll explain everything, then. And no, that man has nothing to do with the agreement I've signed with Max. There was just a misunderstanding. You have nothing to worry about."

Relief swept the young woman's face as she breathed out in a rush. "Great. Awesome," she expanded, as that relief grew. "If you say there's nothing to worry about, then I won't."

Tommi looked at all that spike-haired, near Goth-like sincerity and gave her shoulder another squeeze. "Good. Now, how about we close up and you go on home? As slow as it's been I doubt we'll get any more customers tonight."

She also had a family matter she needed to tend to. Despite her assurances to her waitress, she felt a little sick inside. Part of that had to do with what was—or wasn't—going on with Max. The rest she blamed squarely on Harry Hunt's unmitigated gall.

What her honorary uncle had done had Tommi wavering between feeling insulted, indignant and flat-out incensed. She just had no idea how to deal with the man who was so powerful that his own sons—powerful, wealthy, strong-minded men in their own rights—had bent to his will that *they* marry. She would remain forever grateful to him for the graduation gift that had allowed her to get a foothold on her dream, but no matter who he was, the man had no business messing with her personal life.

She could think of only one person who could even begin to understand how upset she was with their old family friend.

Harry had once set Bobbie up, too.

Forty minutes later, having reached her sister and expended precious energy with some furious scrubbing in her kitchen, she heard Bobbie's hurried "It's me, Tommi!" through the kitchen's open doors.

She'd asked her youngest sibling to let herself in with the backup key she'd given her ages ago. Relieved that support was finally there, she swiped back the hair that had come loose when she'd pulled off her cap, turned the dishwasher on and headed through the doorway. Between her growing unease about Max and her anger with Harry, she couldn't imagine what could possibly make her feel any more upset than she already did. She was, however, about to find out.

Chapter Ten

Shelby had extinguished the glass-cube oil candles on the tables before she'd left, but Tommi'd asked her to leave the house lights on their evening setting. With the overheads dimmed, the three red Italian glass pendants over the bar glowed jewel-like above its black granite surface.

By the center fixture, her sister tossed her coat over a bar stool and opened her arms to give her a hug.

"I'd have been here sooner, but traffic from Bellevue was a nightmare."

Tommi returned her hug, hard. "What were you doing in Bellevue?"

"Getting a new funding grant." Bobbie stepped back, beaming. Her wildly curly nut-brown hair had been tamed as much as it could be by the clip at her nape. Looking totally professional in a charcoal suit, tights and killer heels, she appeared every inch the capable new CEO of Golden Ability Canine Assistance.

"From an organization that doesn't have a single member of the Hunt family on its board to take pity on me," she added proudly.

Even as agitated as she was, Tommi could practically feel her sister's enormous sense of accomplishment. It had taken Bobbie a while—years, actually—but she'd definitely found her niche.

The fact that she was engaged to a great guy and was about to become stepmom to his children put her squarely in her element.

"That's fantastic," Tommi insisted. Crossing her arms over the knots in her stomach, she gave her a smile she feared didn't quite work. "You're going to do great things with that agency. I can tell."

"Thanks, sis, but I feel guilty feeling so good when you obviously don't. Hold on a minute," she said, at the three quick raps on the door. "That'll be Mom. I told her you closed early."

Tommi's heart felt like it stopped, just before it sunk.

"Why did you call Mom?"

She wasn't ready to see her mother, yet. She was wearing the loosest chef's jacket she owned, and the tightest pants she could still fit into. It wasn't as if she thought anyone could look at her and tell she was pregnant. Bobbie certainly hadn't seemed to notice. Neither had her staff, though Alaina had been looking at her rather strangely the past couple of days. Still, as upset as she was with Harry and as concerned as she was trying not to be about Max, the last thing she wanted just then was to risk her mom somehow noticing some…change…about her.

Bobbie was backing toward the door. "Don't be upset with me. I called her because you're almost as big a wimp as I am when it comes to confrontations. In our family, anyway."

"I'm not upset."

"Of course you aren't. You always look like you could debone a chicken with your bare hands."

The knocks at the door gave way to a tap on the window.

"Uncle Harry needs to know he can't be doing this," Bobbie continued, doing an expert dodge and weave between the tables she'd so often served herself. "You know as well as I do that Mom is the only person he'll listen to." Seeing their second to the oldest sister waving from the other side of the glass, Bobbie gave a little start of surprise and, still talking, let her in. "That's why I called her."

"You called Frankie, too?"

"Mom did," their older sibling replied, having hurried in out of the weather. "Hi," she said to Bobbie, buzzing her cheek. "Hey, Tommi. Your decorations look great out there. Love the little trees."

Wiping her narrow-heeled black boots off on the inside mat, Frankie closed out the rain and pushed back the hood of her black London Fog. Her long blond hair gleamed in a high ponytail. Big gold hoop earrings framed her slender neck.

Shedding her coat on her way between the white-clothed tables, dressed in a short sweater and jeans, she looked far more like a student in a sorority than a brainy university research assistant with a Ph.D.

"I was still at work when Mom called. I didn't realize it was so late. I haven't even eaten dinner," she continued, piling her coat and bag on a stool at the end of the bar. "The arrangements for the Master's exhibit at the art museum are taking forever."

The concern in her frown landed on Tommi's undeniably strained features. "It's been since Thanksgiving since we've seen each other," she reminded her with a sisterly hug. "Since she and Georgie are on their way over, Mom thought I should come, too." Her concern deepened. "Mom said Uncle Harry upset you."

Tommi hesitated. Frankie had always had a way with understatements. "Upset" didn't begin to describe it. "Georgie is coming, too?"

"I was going to mention that," Bobbie said. "She was with Mom. They were at Nordstrom."

Frankie's frown changed quality. "Georgie said last week that their Christmas shopping was done."

"I think they were just there because of the sales. You know shopping is sort of their team sport."

"Yeah." The frown turned to a little laugh. "Team Prada. Team Jimmy Choo."

"But 'only on sale,'" Bobbie reminded them, repeating their mother's mantra.

According to Cornelia Fairchild, what the world saw was the quality of the purchase, not the price tag. A woman could look quite tasteful without spending money better invested elsewhere.

Tommi glanced at her own functional rubber clogs. The fact that her work attire left something to be desired on the fashion front barely registered as a blip on her stress screen. Her oldest sister was tapping on the window, announcing that she and their mom needed to be let inside.

It took a minute for coats to be dealt with and hugs to be exchanged among them all. Her mom, her pale blond hair in a neat chignon, looked as slender and elegant as always in a cashmere sweater and matching slacks.

Georgie stood a shade taller than their mother at a statuesque five-feet ten-inches. Every bit as striking as the senior Fairchild, her thick wheat-blond hair flowed loosely down her back. The sweater she wore with her designer jeans was gorgeous. Having just returned from the Sudan, she was on break from her duties for the Hunt Foundation and waiting, somewhat impatiently, Tommi imagined, for her next assignment to some other country or cause in need of her help.

A sociologist with a hunger to ease the plight of others, she clearly felt her younger sister could use her help now. With everyone else still talking by the bar, she turned to where Tommi stood at the end of it.

"So, tell us everything," she began. "Mom said Bobbie told her that Uncle Harry is bribing men to marry you?"

"He *what?*" Frankie looked up from the bag of bar mix she'd pulled from under the granite surface. "You didn't tell me that," she accused. "You just said Harry has caused a problem for Tommi."

"He has," Georgie replied, reasonably. "I didn't see any point in saying anything else when I called because that's all the information I had."

"It's not *men,*" Tommi cut in before Georgie's undeniable logic could provoke a response from the equally logical Frankie. "It was one man. For me, anyway. Bobbie had a lot of strange men leaving messages on her answering machine for a while. For all we know, he could have been bribing them, too.

"What I understood from the man he tried to set me up with is that Harry told him it was time I got married and gave Mom grandchildren...or something like that," she qualified, since those were the exact words Scott had used. "Harry said he'd give him a seat on his board if he married me. Scott said there would be other perks, but he didn't mention what they were."

Her mom had sat down at the table four feet away. A quick frown came and went from her soft features. "This Scott is the man he set you up with?" she asked.

"He is. He's a partner in the firm Harry uses for the

company's land expansions. And, no," she hurried on, in case it was hope and not merely a desire to clarify arching her eyebrows. "I'm definitely not interested."

"I don't believe this." Frankie's need for sustenance gave way to pure indignation. "He actually bribed a man to meet you?"

"He did this to you, too, Bobbie?" their mother asked.

Bobbie had settled on a center stool. "We don't know about the bribing part for sure. Tommi knew he'd set me up with this really...odd—" she decided to call him "—associate of his. It was right after I got him to stop coming by that other men I didn't know started leaving messages on my answering machine." Resting her arm on the bar, her platinum-and-diamond engagement ring flashed in the circle of pendant light. "It was only when she called me tonight that we connected those calls to Harry. There's no other reason for me to have gone a year without a date, then suddenly have offers from total strangers."

Georgie had moved behind the bar. Turning from her perusal of the wine racks, her perfectly shaped eyebrows darted inward. "Did he set you up with Gabe?"

"Oh, good grief, no."

There was more Bobbie could have added to her emphatic denial. The quick glance she darted to Tommi, however, made it clear she didn't care to mention to the rest of them just how desperate she'd been to discourage the man Harry *had* set her up with. Seeing her so-totally-wrong-for-her suitor heading for her porch, she'd grabbed the unsuspecting Gabe by his broad shoulders and laid a lip-lock on him.

As first kisses went, theirs definitely had been unique. But Bobbie hadn't been in love with Gabe when she'd told Tommi what had happened that fateful afternoon.

Truly caring for a man, though, could make seemingly insignificant things far too special to share.

Even as Tommi realized she now understood just how special those little things could be, their first-born sibling gave a disgusted huff.

"Well, he better not try fixing me up with anyone." Looking as adamant as she sounded, Georgie returned to her perusal of the long wine racks. "Just because one of us here is getting married doesn't mean I have any intention of heading down the aisle myself.

"Ever," she pronounced, turning with a bottle of the most expensive red Tommi stocked. She shot a meaningful glance toward her mother. "I'm staying single. I'm perfectly happy with my life just the way it is. Or will be once I get my new assignment," she amended. "Where's a corkscrew? We need wine."

"I'll get the glasses." Every bit as resolute, Frankie joined her behind the bar to line up goblets. "We'll toast independence. No offense, Bobbie," she hurried to add. "I'm thrilled to death for you." She smiled, as sincere in her happiness for what her little sister had found as she was in the desire to protect her own status quo. "Gabe is truly one of a kind. And his kids are terrific. But I can't imagine anything more exciting for me than what I'm doing now."

Tommi had pulled a corkscrew from the utensil tray under the counter. Handing it over, her attention settled on her mother.

Cornelia Fairchild appeared distracted. It also seemed as if she'd barely been listening to her older girls' indignant assertions. As she rose, it appeared as clear as her disquiet that something was gnawing at her in the moments before she began to pace.

Whatever she was thinking had her looking oddly guilty as she toyed with the gold pendant at her throat.

Georgie seemed to notice her strange expression, too, as she offered Tommi a glass of wine.

"No, thanks," Tommi murmured. Uneasily conscious of the way her sister's brow lifted at that refusal, just as conscious of the little life she nurtured inside her, she watched their mother turn to them all.

"I'm afraid some of this may be my fault." Looking from one daughter to the next, that guilt seemed to compound itself. "Harry is so delighted with his daughters-in-law and all his grandchildren. And his sons have seemed so much happier now that they've all settled down," she prefaced. "I just happened to mention in passing how nice it would be for you girls to find good husbands and give me grandchildren, too. But I certainly never thought he'd take the matter into his hands himself," she hurried to defend. "And you have to know that I absolutely do not condone his methods."

Having barreled right over the admission of what Tommi had already suspected, the guilt in her still lovely features moved directly to irritation.

"You all know I thought it unconscionable the way he manipulated his boys into getting married. You know I told him as much, too. I even thought I'd made it quite clear that the end did not justify his means. Just because his sons happened to find lovely girls they adore didn't change the fact that what he did to get them to do his bidding was just plain wrong."

Graceful despite her fury, she accepted the goblet Bobbie handed her. "Bribing men to date my daughters. How dare he."

Like a regal lioness protecting her cubs, she looked to the most recently offended of her den. "I'll take care of this, Tommi," she assured her. "You can be quite certain I'll have my say about how completely unacceptable his actions are. I have no idea how that man's mind works. Believe me, I've tried for years to figure it out. When it comes to relationships, the man hasn't the sense God gave a goat. He plays around with your lives and those of his sons, but does nothing to fix his own. I've waited long enough for him to notice I exist," she insisted. "The next time that nice golf pro at the club asks me out, I'm going."

Everyone but Tommi was taking a sip of what she knew was a superb Brunello. At the seismic shift in their mother's irritation, three sets of eyes widened over rims of crystal. Tommi simply stared in disbelief.

All three of her sisters nearly choked on their wine as their mother finally took a sip of hers.

Since she was the only one who could speak at the moment, Tommi voiced what the others could not.

"You have a thing for Uncle Harry?"

Though her daughters were gaping at her, Cornelia appeared only mildly nonplussed. "Had. Possibly," she admitted, minimizing. "It doesn't matter now. As I said, I'll take care of what he did with the two of you," she continued, with a nod to her youngest daughters. "Since that's resolved, let's just enjoy being together. Someone mentioned a toast. I believe being together is reason enough for one."

When their mother didn't wish to discuss something, she simply...didn't. Having tacitly declared the subject of Uncle Harry off limits, the golf pro she'd mentioned apparently wasn't available for discussion, either.

She'd already lifted her glass. "To my girls."

"To the Fairchild women," said Frankie, only to notice that one of her sisters didn't have anything to raise. "Wait! Tommi needs a glass of wine."

Tommi ducked behind the bar. Not wanting to attract

undue attention, she reached under the lower work surface for a tumbler. "I'll just get some water."

Beside her, she saw Georgie's questioning frown return. "Are you okay?" she asked. "You love good wines."

"Don't you feel well?" Bobbie echoed.

"I'm fine. I'm just…"

I'm just not in the mood for it, she'd started to reply.

"Just tell them," Max had said. *"It'll be like dropping a hundred-pound weight."*

"Pregnant."

With her sisters collectively focused on her, and her mother slowly setting her glass on the table, she now knew this moment wasn't as bad as she'd dreaded.

It was worse.

For a half dozen seconds, the only sound Tommi could hear was the beat of her heart behind her eardrums. Her quiet announcement had produced the same momentarily silencing effect as their mother's admission about their Uncle Harry.

"Pregnant?" Frankie blinked in disbelief. "But you're not even in a relationship!" She hesitated. "Are you?"

Tommi wasn't sure how to answer that. What she and Max shared was too fragile to be defined. After all he'd done for her, after the night they'd shared, she knew only that she wanted—needed—him to be part of her life. Explaining that would only confuse the issue, though. That wasn't the relationship her sister was asking about.

Rolling her eyes, Georgie cut into her awkward silence.

"Oh, Tommi." Georgie always knew exactly what she wanted. She also managed to never let anything stand in her way of reaching whatever that objective was. As Tommi had feared, her hugely accomplished sibling wasted no time voicing disappointment in her apparent lack of that ability.

"What are you going to do with a baby? You barely have this place established. How are you going to keep it up with a child? Are you getting married?"

"Who are you seeing?" Frankie asked, still wanting to know what they'd all apparently missed. "I didn't think you even had time to date."

Before Tommi could even begin to answer the assault of questions, Bobbie rose with the scrape of stool legs against the hardwood floor.

"Ohmygosh, Tommi," she said, wrapping her in a hug. "Oh, wow." Excitement vied with the concern in her voice. "You're going to be the best mom ever. You know that, don't you?" She held her back, looked to Tommi's middle, looked back up. "How far along are you?"

Her sister's faith in her was totally daunting. Tommi just wanted to do the best she could. "Four months."

Her eyes widened. "Why didn't you tell me? You're not even showing! Is it okay? Are you?"

Tommi hugged her back. With her oldest sister looking on with another eye roll, she felt eternally grateful for the support. She also let her first question go. Until Bobbie's life had fallen into place the past few weeks, her little sister had always seemed to have enough problems of her own. As protective as Tommi had always felt of her, it hadn't seemed fair to have her youngest sibling worrying about her, too.

"The baby and I are fine. Really." Placing her hand over her belly to show how little loose fabric there actually was, she gave a shrug. "There's more here than you think.

"And no," she said to Georgie, painfully aware of her censure. "I'm not getting married." Needing to move, Tommi picked up the wine bottle, poured the last few drops into her uncomfortably silent mom's glass. "The father is out of the picture. He's left the country, actually. Which is totally fine," she assured them all. "He was a...mistake," she admitted, seeing no need to elaborate. "As far as I'm concerned, this child is no one's but mine."

The sisterly concern in Georgie surfaced right along with her pragmatism. "That sounds fine," she assured her. "The only thing worse than being married would be marrying the wrong man. But he has a financial obligation to that child. We can't let men just walk away from their responsibilities. Too many women do, you know? You need to assert yourself here, Tommi. At the very least, make whoever he is pay support."

"Absolutely." Frankie dug into the bar mix. "If you don't want anything to do with the guy, I'm behind you a hundred and fifty percent. But educations are expensive. And day care," she added, getting to what came first. "You need good day care to get into good schools."

While Frankie had echoed their mother's philosophy, Georgie had sounded just like Max.

Tommi turned on her heel.

"Where are you going?" Georgie wanted to know.

"To get Frankie something to eat. She missed dinner."

"We could go after him," she could hear Frankie saying. Her voice rose. "What country did he go to?" she called as Tommi disappeared through the open kitchen doors.

"It doesn't matter," she called back, grabbing a plate from the rack.

Frankie remained undeterred. "We can find out and go after him," she insisted, but whatever else she said was lost as Tommi took the chill off leftover chicken confit for her, heated bread in the microwave and put together a plate of pâté and brie for the rest of them.

"Still taking care of your sisters?"

Her mom's quiet voice drifted over the muffled sounds of her two oldest siblings speculating, debating and otherwise deciding her options. Bobbie, as usual, wisely stayed out of the debate.

Glancing over her shoulder at her mom, Tommi gave her a strained little shrug. "Frankie should eat. I thought everyone else might like something, too."

She returned to her task. It was easier than looking at all the disappointment she'd known she'd see in her mom's eyes.

The concern so apparent there didn't make her feel any better.

"You know, Tommi," her mom began, folding the napkin over the basket of warm bread, "if you're already four months along it's apparent this happened before I made that remark to Harry. And I can't imagine that you'd have said anything to him before you told us, so his trying to get you married is just coincidental.

"All that aside, I'm not going to ask you for any details," she assured her. "You're a grown woman and I'm sure you have your reasons for not wanting to discuss the father. That's not my concern right now, anyway.

"I haven't always agreed with the choices you've made," she admitted, reminding Tommi all over again of how upset she'd been when Tommi had applied to culinary school instead of to university, "but I need you to know that this truly isn't what I wanted for you.

"I'm not talking about your bistro." She touched Tommi's arm to keep her from turning away. "I know you love doing what you do. If this makes you happy and you can take care of yourself doing it, then that's really all that matters to me. What worries me is how you'll take care of yourself. And a baby. I raised the four of you without any help after your father died. I know how hard it is to do this on your own. So, what I need to know now is how you'll keep up. Most of the time, you work sixteen hours a day. Your reviews are wonderful. And I'm so proud of you for that. But I also know you haven't taken a vacation in three years. You can't keep up that pace now. You need more help."

For the first time in the last few months, Tommi actually felt some of the burden she'd carried lift from her shoulders.

Thanks to Max, this was the easy part.

"Everything here is under control, Mom." She offered the assurance with a sort of certainty she hadn't felt in a very long time. "I've already hired a new sous chef. He starts next month," she told her, looking back to the plate she prepared. "I worked with him and his wife in culinary school. She's a pastry chef. She may be coming to work for me, too.

"I'm expanding the bistro into the space next door," she continued, tucking a few cornichons next to the pâté. "Since that will more than double my seating, I'll be hiring even more help."

Surprise tempered concern. "You can do that? Expand, I mean?"

"Yeah, Mom." She looked up with a small smile. "I can. I've taken on a partner who even wants to franchise my concept. That's at least a year or so away. But it's in my plans. As for raising this baby on my own, I know it won't be easy. But I have an excellent example to follow.

"So you know what?" she asked, watching her compliment sink in. "We're just going to look at the bright side. You wanted grandchildren. Between mine and Bobbie's new stepchildren, you'll soon have three of them. And for what it's worth," she added, her throat going a little tight at the sheen of tears her mom blinked back with a smile, "I'm sure certain of my sisters will be more than happy to let me know if I'm doing something wrong."

"I only mention problems," claimed Georgie, clearly

having overheard as she walked in, "because I want what's best for you. You know I'll support you any way I can. But do you think expanding right now is a good idea? Shouldn't you be getting more rest instead of taking on such a big project?"

"Expanding what?" Frankie asked, in search of whatever her sister the chef was conjuring up for her.

Bobbie poked her head through the doorway. "I'm pouring you sparkling water. Okay?"

Telling Bobbie that would be great, she handed Frankie the bowl of confit she'd prepared and Georgie the bread. Picking up the appetizer plate herself, she ushered them all back out to where Bobbie took over the back of the bar.

As it tended to do when they were together, conversation bounced all over the place. But as it jumped from the expansion of her bistro to the need for baby furnishings, which led to her mentioning her move to the bigger apartment, then on to the plans for Bobbie's wedding right after Christmas, Tommi found herself still listening for the ring of the phone.

It was because of Max that she'd been able to assure her family that she did, indeed, have everything under control. Thanks to him, too, she was actually feeling the first flickers of excitement over the changes she was about to make. The expansion suddenly seemed more daring than daunting. Except for when it came to food, she'd never felt daring in her life.

Because of him, she was now thinking outside the little box she lived in. She would be making changes she'd mentally fought, but which would allow her to expand in the culinary world she loved. There was something exciting about that growth; something she could actually feel in her smile. Or maybe her smile came more easily now because, for the first time, too, she could feel excitement mingling with her lengthening list of anxieties about all the ways she could mess up a child.

Yet, "under control" was not how she felt when it came to Max himself. She seemed to have no power over how important he'd become to her. But no matter how she felt about him, she had the awful feeling he might never be able to love her back.

Chapter Eleven

Max had spent the first of the week in Chicago straightening out a client's zoning problem during the day, and evenings with their office manager discussing personnel options for New York. Just because Scott didn't care to be involved in an expansion didn't mean Max wasn't going to proceed. Ninety percent of the company's growth wouldn't have happened if he'd let Scott dictate its direction.

The leasing agent in New York had two new office spaces for him to check out. Having left Chicago for his meeting in San Jose, and only now returning to Seattle, he greeted Margie with a preoccupied smile and the request to get him on a morning flight to LaGuardia. He'd just left her desk when he walked into his office to find the L&C file for Tommi's bistro on his chair with a note from Scott.

His partner had written the note on a sheet from a yellow legal pad and clipped it to the front. Behind it were the two copies of the unsigned agreement from the envelope

Max had thrown into the file when he'd grabbed what he'd needed to take with him last Monday.

Anyone reading the message would think it nothing more than a communication between the two partners. Max, however, didn't miss an iota of the sarcasm, resentment and revenge in the man's bold scrawl.

Nice work. Really appreciate the way you handled things with Tommi Fairchild. I repaid the favor. She knows what kind of returns you're after.

A quick call to Scott's secretary revealed that he had already left for the weekend. For Aspen.

A call to his BlackBerry went to voice mail.

Max hung up his desk phone.

His frustration with his partner had moved to something infinitely less benign when he'd come up against Scott's apathy and lack of conscience last week. His disgust with the man now rose with his latest offenses—not the least of which was that the guy had gone through his office. That file had been in his bottom desk drawer.

There was only one thing that concerned Max at the moment, though. Yet he really didn't want the jerk's take on how Tommi had reacted to whatever it was he'd said to her.

He'd find out for himself.

He needed to see her, anyway.

At the heavy double knock on the bistro's back door, Tommi's glance flew to the security monitor near the wall clock. Within seconds of recognizing Max's image on the screen, she'd darted across the kitchen and pushed the door open.

Knowing he was due back, she'd felt as if she'd been holding her breath since dawn.

"Hi," she said, her smile cautious.

"Hi, yourself."

His features were as guarded as his voice as he stepped into the warmth of the narrow space. Closing out the rain as she backed up, he looked straight to where the lights beyond the kitchen doors had been turned off for the afternoon, then to the ovens filling the room with aromas savory and sweet.

His jaw was working as his glance finally settled on her.

"Is anyone else here?"

She gave a quick shake of her head. "Alaina just left. The Olsons aren't due for another hour."

Raindrops clung to his dark hair, beaded on the wide shoulders of his open overcoat. She wanted nothing more than to have him walk up to her and wrap her in his arms. But that wasn't what he seemed to have in mind as he took off his coat and tossed it over a stool a few feet away.

Muscle-knotting tension radiated from him in waves, grazing nerves already jumpy just seeing him again. That agitation seemed to be doing battle with something far less definable as he carefully searched her face.

"Max, what's wrong?"

He stepped closer. "What did Scott say to you?"

The quick anxiety she'd felt leaked out like air from a punctured tire.

A moment ago, she hadn't known what to make of the fierce edge in his expression. Now, her own tension fading, she realized that that edge had a decidedly self-protective feel about it. He obviously had some idea of what his partner had told her. He just didn't know how she'd taken it.

"More than he'd first intended, I think. But everything's okay." She offered the assurance with a soft smile. "It would have been nice if he'd checked his email before he'd come here," she conceded. "That way he'd have known I'm working with you and not the company. But if he hadn't come by, I wouldn't have known about Uncle Harry's bribe."

With his brow furrowing at her logic, she tipped her head, hoping it was just his uncertainty about what she'd been told holding him back from her. She couldn't believe how badly she'd missed him.

"I take it he told you why Hunt set you up with him?"

"He did."

"Did he tell you I was out to collect on that bribe?"

"Not in so many words. But he did make it sound as if that was why you'd offered to be my partner."

"And?"

She shrugged. "He doesn't know you as well as he believes he does."

It took a moment, but the tightness in his jaw seemed to change quality. As if debating whether or not he wanted to touch her, or maybe, if he should, he finally lifted his hand to her cheek.

"Just so you know, I didn't have any ulterior motives with you, Tommi. You do know that. Right?"

He was talking about more than the document they'd signed. There was no doubt of that in her mind as his eyes held hers. Though something about his use of the past tense bothered her, she didn't believe for an instant that he'd tried to maneuver his way into her bed. It seemed he needed to be sure she understood that.

Heat gathered where his fingers skimmed her cheek; partly from his gentle caress, partly from the memory of how she'd all but begged him not to let her go. "Of course I do. I've never thought otherwise."

Her head unconsciously turned to his touch. The movement was barely perceptible, but it caused something to shift in the tense lines of his face.

As if memorizing the feel of her skin, he let his fingers drift to her jaw. "That's good to know," he murmured, and let his hand fall.

"So," he continued, taking a step back to push his hands into the front pockets of his slacks. "What are you going to do about your uncle?"

Confused by his touch, more than a little uneasy with the deliberate distance he'd created, she focused on the concern in his voice.

"Mom will take care of Uncle Harry. She was pretty upset when we told her what was going on."

"We?"

"Bobbie and I. We think he set her up, too. I'd called her after Scott left," she explained, because he clearly wanted details. "She thought we needed to bring Mom in on it, since she's the only one who really knows how to deal with him."

"You called your mother?"

"Actually, she came here. She was with my oldest sister when Bobbie called her, so one call led to another and pretty soon my whole family was out there at the wine bar."

Nothing in the uneasy way she watched him gave Max a clue about how that little scenario had played out. The disquiet he knew was there because of him overshadowed the reactions that would have otherwise been easy for him to read. He wanted badly to reach for her again, to make that disquiet go away. But that relief would only be temporary for both of them, and he had no business thinking about anything other than what he'd come there to resolve.

His first intention after reading Scott's note had been to make sure she hadn't believed he was out to use her in any way. Her comment about her family had led straight to the next concern on his list.

He didn't know if it was because the chef's jacket she wore had become more snug since he'd last seen her wearing one, or because he was intimately familiar with the betraying curve of her belly. But he couldn't look at her now and not be conscious of the baby she carried.

For a few unguarded moments, in the heat of their love-making, he'd almost wished that child was his.

"Your family was all here," he prefaced, banishing the unwanted memory. "Did you tell them?"

She didn't have to ask what he meant. "I did."

"How did they take the news?"

"With varying degrees of acceptance. But it's going to be okay," she allowed, a hint of a smile surfacing. "Bobbie's excited and Mom's getting that way. And you were right. I do feel better now that I've told them."

"What about your staff?"

"They know, too," she continued. "I told them in our meeting yesterday when I explained our initial plans to expand. They were wonderful about everything. It was a little awkward at first, because they know I wasn't going out with anyone. But I just told them what I told my family…that the father is gone." Her eyes sought his as her voice dropped. "You're the only one who knows about him. Okay?"

She was asking that he protect what she'd shared with no one else.

Honoring that confidence was the very least he could do.

"Of course."

"Thank you," she said quietly, and tried for another smile.

Had she been anyone else, Max knew he would have let his absence and his silence of the past few days speak for itself. When it came to personal relationships, he'd learned to never give a woman reason to expect anything more from him than what was mutually beneficial at the time. He always made it clear from the start that he had no expectations where she was concerned. More important, he never mixed business with sex.

Despite the fact that he'd broken every one of those rules with the woman cautiously watching him, he hadn't been able to just walk away. He'd done what he could for her business. But he'd wanted to know she would be okay with her family. Knowing that they and her staff now knew about her baby and would be there for them, he could let that concern go.

As for how she'd taken what Harry Hunt had done, he couldn't help being impressed by the way her family had banded together for her. He wasn't familiar with that kind of backing, but it seemed to be the very sort of support she needed.

She had family. She had friends. She and her child would be fine.

"Listen," he said, knowing it was time to let go of it all. "I'm moving to New York to set up a base for my own holding company. Scott doesn't know it yet, but we're splitting up the partnership. The break has been a long time coming," he conceded, not wanting her to think she was responsible for that. Not totally, anyway.

"I'll be in Seattle on and off for a while, but just to take care of splitting up the operation." He hadn't had time to work through that quagmire. He just knew he'd make it happen. "Since our agreement is separate from all of that, if you have any problems with my accountant or J.T.'s assistant, call me on my cell and I'll make sure Margie sees it's taken care of."

She'd thought she was prepared. She'd thought that having told herself he might never be able to feel about her the way she did about him would have somehow equipped her for what she was hearing now.

She'd been wrong. Because of all he'd done for her, because of how he'd been there for her, hope had loomed too large for the warnings to have provided any protection at all.

Scott had said something about Max's personal portfolio. Remembering that, she didn't know which hurt the most just then; that Max was done with her now that she'd been acquired, or that he was staffing her out.

Desperate to hide that hurt, she turned away.

She hadn't turned fast enough.

"Tommi, I'm sorry." Max caught her by the arm, then swore under his breath when she pulled back and stepped from his reach. "I never intended for things to go as far as they did between us. And I never said I'd be around after we signed our—"

"Max, don't. Please." Taking another step back, she held up her hand as if to physically halt the words. She didn't need to have him tell her he'd never intended to get involved with her the way he had. She especially didn't need to hear him say that what had been so emotionally significant to her had been a mistake. What she did need was to keep them both from saying anything they would have to regret. She might be little more to him than a small investment he wouldn't personally oversee, but he was still a partner in her business.

"I'm not asking anything of you," she defended. "So please don't make it sound as if I am. I don't expect anything from you other than what's in our agreement." It was painfully clear he didn't want her thinking he'd be there for her in any way other than financially. She didn't need him to verbalize that, either. "We have a silent partnership," she reminded him, not feeling anywhere near as strong as she hoped she sounded. "So what happened between us is something we'll just stay silent about."

Feeling every bit as defensive as he now looked, she watched him take a shoulder-raising breath and shove his fingers through his hair. She didn't know if he was relieved by her solution or frustrated by it. As he let his hand fall, all she knew for certain was that whatever internal chaos he was dealing with was hardly due entirely to her.

"I'm sorry about what's going on with you and your partner, Max." Her defenses where he was concerned had finally shown up, but she knew what it was to have certain fundamentals in her life change whether she liked the idea or not. With his partnership somehow forced into breaking up, he could well be feeling that upheaval. Especially since he had chosen to add the pressure of opening a new office on top of it all.

She had the feeling, though, that he welcomed what would have only compounded her stress.

"But mostly," she added, "I'm sorry you haven't found whatever it is you're looking for. Or that you haven't run far enough away from whatever it is you're trying to escape."

His dark eyebrows darted into a single slash. "What are you talking about?"

"That thing that drives you," she said quietly. For her, it had always been the need for security. Having grown up as he had, for all she knew, that could be what drove him, too. "I don't know if you push yourself so hard with work because you're looking for something, or running away from it. Whichever it is, I suspect it won't let you stay still long enough to enjoy whatever it is you have at the moment." The thrill of the acquisition undoubtedly provided its own sort of rush. She just had a hard time believing he found any contentment in it. "For your sake, I hope you figure it out."

He was cheating himself of so much. Acutely conscious of his withdrawal from her as he picked up his coat, she was as certain of that as she was the knot of hurt living just below her heart.

"Don't worry about me, Tommi. I'm fine with what I do."

There was nothing for him to figure out. Max felt utterly convinced of that as he pulled on his overcoat. He had the life he wanted. Heaven knew he'd worked hard enough to attain it. Even the breakup of his partnership didn't threaten him the way she did. He'd seen companies split and parcel out into bigger and better operations. He'd steered some of those clients on to even more lucrative paths himself. But she'd been poking at the foundations of the carefully constructed life he'd so deliberately built pretty much since he'd met her.

"I have to go." He hated the way she'd pulled from him before. Certain she'd only do it again, knowing he'd lost any right he had to touch her, he moved to the back door so she wouldn't have to lock the front behind him. "You take care of yourself."

Tightening her grip on her arms, she gave a little nod. "You, too."

He turned then, walking away from the wounded look in her eyes and the brave little smile she'd clearly hoped would mask it. His defenses locked and loaded, he wouldn't let himself consider the odd little void opening in his chest. He just let himself out, drove off and waited for the sense of reprieve he'd fully expected to feel.

The relief didn't come that day, though.

Or the next.

Still, his sense of self-preservation insisted that it would come. He just needed to get to New York to look at those offices, and sign the notice of intent he'd had his attorney draw up about the split Scott had to know was coming. Once he was buried in work, he was sure the void would disappear.

Christmas Eve had once been Tommi's favorite time of year. That had been when her family had gone to services together, then returned home for a festive supper before she and her sisters would each open one gift—which, suspiciously, always turned out to be pajamas. Their parents and, later, her mom, had saved the main opening of presents for Christmas morning. But the eve had always seemed like a big present in itself; the official beginning of what all the preparation had been about.

It was just now six o'clock, but she could have already joined Bobbie and her almost-new family for whatever traditions they would create that evening. Or gone to her mom's where her other sisters would be helping with preparations for Christmas dinner.

Instead, hating that she felt so empty when she had so much to be grateful for, Tommi had made a mental leap past Christmas altogether and focused on Bobbie's wedding the day after. On the cake, anyway. She missed the man she'd so carelessly fallen in love with far too much to think about the more romantic aspects of the event. Missed him, wished she'd never met him, and felt hugely grateful to him for the funding and ideas for her business that she'd never have considered on her own.

The bistro was closed. It had been all day. And all day, she had been mixing and baking layers of carrot, chocolate and orange gateau. The combination would have sent food critics into a culinary tailspin, but it perfectly suited her sister's sometimes indecisive, always eclectic tastes.

With the layers baked and in the freezer because they were easier to frost frozen, she was working on the roughly two hundred royal icing snowflakes that would cascade down tiers of buttercream when her cell phone chimed.

Thinking it would be her mom checking to see if she'd made enough progress to change her mind about coming over, she wiped her fingers, dug beneath her apron and pulled her cell phone from the pocket of her gray sweatpants. The beauty of having the day off and working alone was that she could work in comfort. She hadn't even bothered with makeup.

"Since I had to call your cell, I take it you're not home."

At the sound of Max's voice, her pulse gave an unhealthy jerk. "I'm in the bistro."

He hesitated. "The bistro is closed."

"How do you know that?"

"What are you doing there?" he asked, ignoring the question. "When you didn't answer your home phone, I figured you were out doing whatever it is people do the night before Christmas."

He knew the bistro was closed. There was only one way he could know that for certain.

With her phone to her ear, she pulled off her apron and walked into the dark dining area, letting the door swing closed behind her. Without illumination from the kitchen, the only light in the interior came from the glow of tiny white lights outlining the front and side windows and the rows of little trees in the planters below them.

"I'm working on my sister's wedding cake," she said, moving between the pale shapes of the cloth-draped tables. "She's getting married the day after tomorrow." She looked out the front window. Icy rain blew at an angle through the halos of the streetlamps as she scanned the cars parked along the curbs.

His black Mercedes coupe was there. But he wasn't in it.

"Where are you?" she asked.

She couldn't help the hesitation in her tone. Or the hope she didn't want to feel. Knowing his penchant for working through weekends and evenings, and having encountered his ambivalence about the holidays, it was entirely probable that he was there on business.

After the walls he'd thrown up before he'd walked out six days and roughly three hours ago, not that she'd kept track, she just couldn't imagine what he wanted that couldn't have been accomplished by messenger or telephone.

"Max?" she asked.

"I'm here. I'm coming around back."

She lifted the Closed shade to see him walking toward the bistro, his dark hair whipping in the wind, his cell phone to his ear.

He must have been in the entryway to her apartment building in the middle of the block. Noticing the movement of the shade, he slowed his pace. A heartbeat later, she saw him lower his phone just before her connection went dead.

Dropping her own phone back into her pocket, she had the door open by the time he reached it to let him in from the cold.

The freezing air came in with him, making her shiver before she locked out the chill and turned to where he'd stopped six feet away. In the silvery illumination of the lights twinkling through the window, she watched him push his fingers through the dampness glinting in his hair. With his dark parka open in seeming defiance of the weather, he looked very large, very commanding and, even in that shadowy light, almost as tense as she suddenly felt.

"I won't keep you," he promised. "Since you have family, I figured I'd have a better chance finding you home tonight than I would tomorrow. I just wanted to give you this."

From his jacket's inner pocket, he withdrew what looked like rolled paper tied with a shiny ribbon.

It was too dark to see what it was where they stood. Taking what he'd handed her, she moved to the wine bar and flipped the switch that illuminated the red pendants and white spots over its gleaming granite surface. In that soft light, she slipped off the thin silver ribbon and uncurled two sheets of paper.

One was a photocopy of a real estate offer and acceptance. The other, a copy of a memo to someone named Alissa Arnold, Esq.

Her glance caught on "Partial transfer of title to Thomasina Grace Fairchild" in the subject line.

That was as far as she got before, puzzled, she looked up.

"What is this?"

"It's the first Christmas present I've given anyone on my own in about twenty years." The corporate stuff didn't count. That was business. Though this had to do with her business, as far as Max was concerned, it was strictly personal. "I'm sorry I can't give you the actual deed yet. But I didn't realize what I wanted to give you until a few days ago." Four days ago, to be exact, when he'd been standing in the middle of a prime piece of Manhattan real estate wondering when what he had would ever be enough.

"The deal still has to close," he explained, "and there will be some legal work involved separating out parts of the property, but that first page shows that my offer on this building has been accepted. Margie found out it was for sale when I asked her to go ahead with the lease for the space next door. I didn't know what another buyer would do with it, so I called from New York on Monday and bought it myself.

"That second copy," he said as her mouth fell open, "is a memo to my attorney about deeding the bistro, the space next door and the top floor to you. You need a bigger place, so I'll put in an elevator and convert all that unused space to a penthouse. That way you'll have room for a nanny. Since you'll own it outright, you won't have to pay any more rent."

She sank to a stool at the middle of the bar. "You're giving this all to me…for Christmas?"

Her caution had merged with disbelief and no small amount of confusion. Max felt pretty sure that confusion existed for a number of reasons. Not the least of which was his acknowledgment of a holiday that had held no joy for him in longer than he'd cared to remember.

But he had remembered, anyway. She'd more or less made it impossible not to.

"I thought I'd try it your way. You said it took a long time after you lost your father to really look forward to the holidays," he reminded her. "But seeing everyone else happy made you happy, too. I think I'm beginning to see how that works."

He'd done what he had because he wanted what she'd found.

Apparently realizing that, something soft tempered the disbelief in her expression. "But you bought the whole building?"

His shrug wasn't anywhere near as casual as it appeared. "I decided not to move to New York. I'm just going to see what plays out splitting the partnership and concentrate on investments like this. I know how you feel about your neighbors and how they feel about all the condominium conversions around here. You can tell Syd he can stop worrying. The apartments won't be converted to condos."

The papers she held had curled back into themselves. Holding them in one hand, she clasped them to the soft fleece between her breasts..

"Oh, Max. Thank you for that. And for this," she added, folding her free hand over the other to clutch his gift more tightly. She opened her mouth, closed it again.

In the subtle lighting, her skin looked as pale and smooth as alabaster, her features as delicate as a cameo. Without makeup, her hair in a careless knot and wearing a sweatshirt that looked big enough to swallow her whole, she looked more like a child than a woman who would soon have one. Torn between the need to touch her and the need to pace, he opted for the latter. The last time he'd reached for her, she'd pulled back from him. The last thing he wanted was to ruin what he was trying to do.

"There's one more thing." His motivations had been unfamiliar, but discussing property had kept him close to his comfort zone. About to move light years beyond it, he clamped his hand over the muscles knotted at the back of his neck.

"I blew off what you said about something driving me. But the more I tried to not think about it, the harder it got to convince myself you were wrong."

He walked to the end of the bar, turned when he reached it. "You said you didn't know if I was looking for something or running away from it.

"I know which it is," he admitted, torn between a lifetime of self-defense and the need to let some of it go. He'd always known. He just hadn't considered what it had cost him until she'd caused him to face what he now stood to lose. "I've spent the last twenty years of my life running from the first eighteen."

He had wanted to move as far and as fast as he could from the life of struggle he'd grown up with. He'd allowed her glimpses of that life, grudgingly, and with as little detail as possible, so he'd never told her how he hated never knowing a real home of his own back then.

He now owned four, two of which he set foot in only when he took clients to Aspen or Carmel.

He hadn't mentioned that, growing up, they'd never had a car.

He now collected them. He had a Cobra, two Jags and an Aston Martin lined up like trophies in a climate-controlled garage on his Carmel estate, attended by his caretakers there.

He belonged to yacht and country clubs. He had a sailing sloop and interests in hotels and restaurants he once never could have afforded to stay or eat in, and companies that produced goods he never could have afforded to buy.

He brushed past those details, though, as he paced past her, still working at the knots. They weren't important. What was so significant to him was the insight of the woman who apparently knew him better than he'd known himself. It was because of her that he'd found himself in a room at the Plaza making a list of his acquisitions and discovered that much of what he owned were things he'd all but forgotten, took for granted, rarely used or otherwise ignored. It had been the next morning, in the processes of preparing to acquire more in the form of an office he didn't need that her words had slammed his priorities into place.

Whichever it is, I suspect it won't let you stay still long enough to enjoy whatever it is you have at the moment.

"I've spent all those years getting more. More property,

more money, more possessions. More business," he had to add, since that was what allowed it all. "But you were right. I don't enjoy what I have. I just get it, get out and move on."

Because there was always more to be had, more to store up, more to keep him from winding up like his mom— or like one of the homeless guys the kindhearted woman quietly watching him occasionally fed. His need to never know that spiraling lack of control had driven him ever since.

"So now I have everything I could possibly want." Coming to a halt a foot in front of her, he dropped his head, rubbed at his neck again. He hated the thought of what that need for control may have cost him. "Except for what you showed me is missing.

"I'd like a chance to start over with you, Tommi. I know I'm coming at you out of the blue on this, but I think we have something worth working on. And you have a baby that could use a dad. Maybe you'll let me help."

It had never taken him so long to get to a point. But now that he had, he'd jumped right over so much of what else she needed to know. He needed her to know she'd become essential to him somehow, necessary in ways he hadn't realized existed. He needed to tell her he was new at all this and that he'd already gotten ahead of himself.

Mostly, he needed to know what she was about to say as she looked up at him as if she didn't trust what she was hearing.

Tommi's heart bumped her breastbone. From the moment he had stunned her with the gift that had been huge as much for its significance as its size, he'd left her trying to grasp everything from the fact that he wasn't moving away to how profoundly his past still affected him. And all that was before he'd asked for another chance with her.

"You want to help with the baby?"

Taking the papers from her other hand, he set them on the bar behind her. "Yeah. I do," he murmured, his glance caressing her face as he traced the line of her jaw with his knuckles. "I want a lot of things. But I don't want to rush you. Right now, I just want to know if I have that chance."

He needed her. He wanted to give her time to need him, too. Drawn by that implausible realization, the hope she hadn't wanted to feel pushed hard. "That might depend on what else you want."

She'd turned slightly into his touch. He was more relieved by that unconscious acceptance of him than he'd have thought possible. Yet, he could almost feel her self-protectiveness, too. Until last week, that defense hadn't been there. Not with him. "Are you negotiating?" he asked, hating what he caused her to feel. "Or just curious."

"Both," she quietly admitted.

He'd already leapt ahead on his wish list. Figuring she had to have at least some idea of where he was headed, he decided to start with the smaller things and work his way back up.

"I want different memories of Christmas than what I have." He already had a few new ones, thanks to her. He gathered a few more as he breathed in the scent of vanilla mingling with herbal shampoo and absorbed the soft feel of her skin beneath his fingers.

"And I want to take care of you. And be there for you."

His voice dropped, turned a little husky. "I want the family I didn't think I needed until I met you. And I want you to not worry about your baby not having a father. If it would make things easier to get married before the baby is born, it can have my name. If you need more time, I'll adopt later. Like I said, I don't want to rush you into anything. If that's not what you want, then we'll just work together on whatever parts you do.

"I'm no prince, Tommi. I have no practice at any of this. Not with the words. Not with any of it. I don't know if it'll even make sense, but there's a hole inside me without you." Feeling totally exposed, he eased his hand away. "So I hope I wasn't just imagining that you cared about me, too."

The sides of his heavy jacket lay open wide over his charcoal pullover. Lifting her hand to his broad chest, Tommi rested her palm over the strong beat of his heart. Her own beat so hard she could barely breathe.

"You didn't imagine it, Max. I fell in love with you," she said, the simple truth breaking free. "And what you said about the hole makes perfect sense."

She knew that empty space. But hers filled to overflowing as something like reprieve shifted in the carved lines of his face in the seconds before he tugged her to her feet. He smelled of cold, rain and wonderfully warm male as he pulled her arms inside his jacket.

The tension that always lurked beneath his easy smiles seemed to seep right out of him. Intimately familiar with his own calming effect on her, it touched her deeply to know that what she'd found in his touch, he'd found in hers, too.

"You know something," he said, looking oddly humbled. "I have a really limited frame of reference for what love is supposed to be. But if part of it is needing all the things I want with you, then I love you, too."

She tipped her head, her sunshine smile in her eyes. "I'm good with that. And it won't be just you taking care of me. We'll take care of each other. Okay?"

"Deal," he murmured, and covered her smile with his. Slipping her arms around his neck, Tommi kissed him back, her knees going weak at the possession, tenderness and promise in his embrace. He loved her. He wanted to marry her. He wanted her child.

Overwhelmed by the gifts he was giving her, she was fully prepared to let him continue kissing her breathless when he lifted his dark head.

"You said you were working on something down here. How long before you're finished?"

"I can finish tomorrow," she insisted, only to remember that half the day was already accounted for.

"What?" he asked, at the pinch of her eyebrows.

Aligned the length of his long, hard body, she tipped her head.

"You said you wanted some different memories of Christmas," she reminded him. "I have to go to Mom's for dinner tomorrow. How do you feel about being thrown into the deep end of the pool?"

"What time would we have to be there?"

"Not until two."

He lifted his hand, glanced over her shoulder at his watch. Something devilish glinted in his eyes as he lowered his head once more "That gives us about nineteen hours," he murmured, and pulled her right back to where she'd wanted to be pretty much since the moment they'd met.

She had been raised to never believe in the fairy tale. And he'd claimed to be no prince. Yet, what she'd discovered was that rescues went both ways, and that there was something pretty special about being loved by the knight in shining armor she got for Christmas.

Epilogue

Bobbie's wedding was exactly as she wanted it—unconventional and disorganized as it undoubtedly appeared to some of those present. Where most of the Fairchild women's tastes were infinitely more sophisticated and traditional, Tommi's oft-bohemian little sister's were decidedly...not.

There had been no formal procession, no organ music, no aisle to traverse. It was just the bride, looking enchanting in a long, flowing slip of palest pink gossamer with streaming ribbons at her bare shoulders, the man she loved, his children and Tommi standing in front of the minister. Gathered around them were those Bobbie cared about most: her and Gabe's families, two golden retrievers and a few close friends.

The fact that she was being married in front of a twenty-foot silver-and-white Christmas tree in the center of a soaring ballroom was incidental.

The room had been decorated for Uncle Harry's annual

holiday party tomorrow night. Since there hadn't been enough room at their mother's to comfortably hold the two dozen guests—especially with Gabe's children, the Hunt brothers' preschoolers and toddlers and two rambunctious dogs needing room to roam—Bobbie had taken their Uncle Harry up on his offer to hold the ceremony at his huge, sprawling house on the lake.

That had been before Tommi had discovered Harry's attempts to take her and Bobbie's futures into his own hands. After their mother's talk with him, though, he had phoned them each personally to insist that he'd had only their best interests at heart. He'd also asked Bobbie to keep her wedding at his home. He wanted to talk to Cornelia, but she wasn't taking his calls.

It seemed their mother still wasn't speaking to him. As far as Tommi knew, she hadn't even made eye contact with the six-foot-six-inch-tall, distinguished-looking gentleman in the black horn-rimmed glasses standing with his sons and their wives and the other guests gathered around the tree.

Having been long acquainted with J. T. Hunt and his brother Gray, Max stood to one side with them. As her sister and Gabe exchanged their vows, Tommi could practically feel Max's eyes on the back of the emerald green empire dress skimming her expanding belly.

Max had met Bobbie and Gabe's family yesterday at Christmas dinner, along with Georgie, Frankie and their mom.

Her mother, gracious as always, had immediately welcomed him as her new business partner. So had her sisters. Though he'd only touched her to help her with her coat and her chair, it hadn't been long before her mom had started watching them more closely—and giving her looks that said she'd noticed how he couldn't seem to keep his eyes off her.

Tommi had figured that was because she'd kept watching him herself. Since Christmas dinner at the Fairchild home was his first adult experience with a true family holiday gathering, she'd wanted to know what he thought of it. Mostly, she'd wanted to know if he felt the simple joy she did sharing something with him that he hadn't celebrated in a very long time.

She'd loved the easy way he'd smiled at her, and how his interest in her sisters and their guests had drawn them in. She'd especially loved how intrigued he'd been by the children who'd added a whole new dimension to the otherwise adult affair with their excitement as they'd opened packages by the tree, their constant questions and their youthful energy.

That energy now had Gabe's young son fidgeting with his tie even as the minister said, "I now pronounce you husband and wife. You may kiss your bride."

Beside her, Tommi overheard Gabe softly whisper "I love you" to her sister an instant before applause erupted.

As full as her own heart felt, still wrestling with hormones that bounced all over the place, that private declaration had her throat going tight. She wasn't totally sure what all else they'd said to each other as they'd spoken her vows. Her focus had been on not letting herself cry, and on the man whose eyes she now sought.

While everyone else moved forward to congratulate the new Mr. and Mrs. Gabriel Gannon, Max headed toward her.

Tall, broad-shouldered, big, he looked impossibly handsome to her in his collarless black shirt and tailored black suit. Holding her knot of surprisingly traditional red roses, thinking how easily he fit here among her family, she saw his silver blue eyes smile as his glance drifted over her face.

"They're opening the bar, if you want something," she said, feeling as if he'd touched her, wishing he would.

"What I want isn't at the bar. Let's stay here for minute." As if he'd read her mind, he slipped his fingers somewhat protectively—or maybe it was possessively—through hers and tugged her away from the sudden din of conversation and no-longer-curtailed children. "I have something for you."

With the bride and groom now working their way toward the beautifully set tables by the windows overlooking the lake, everyone else following, he led her around the massive tree to block them from view.

"You were still busy with the snowflakes when I came back to pick you up," he told her, reaching into his slacks' pocket. She'd put the last details on the multitiered cake while he'd gone home to shower and change clothes. "So I didn't have a chance to give you this."

He opened a small blue box. She barely caught a glimpse of something dark and glittery inside before he took it out. With a snap, the box closed and he dropped it back into his pocket.

"Whenever you feel ready to make it official, we can pick out your engagement ring together." He picked up her left hand and slipped an exquisite marquise sapphire onto her third finger. The diamonds and platinum surrounding it winked in the lights from the tree as he lifted her knuckles to his lips. "This is just a belated Christmas gift."

He brought her hand to his chest, held it to his heart. Blinking at the beautiful ring, her own heart squeezed. He'd already given her so much.

"When did you get this?"

"On my way back to your place this afternoon. I'd seen

it in a hotel window in New York, so I called the hotel yesterday morning while you were still asleep. The jeweler overnighted it. I had it sent to Margie's house so she could sign for it."

Yesterday had been Christmas. Half the world had been closed. Yet, just like that, he'd gotten what he wanted. From the other side of the country. For her.

With her heart smiling, she looped her arms around his neck.

"I love it, Max. I love you," she stressed. "But I already got my Christmas present. He showed up on my doorstep Christmas Eve.

"As for making it official," she said, nodding her head to the people she'd just noticed out of the corner of her eye, "I think you just did."

He'd slipped his arms around her, the feel of them as wonderfully familiar as the delicious darkening in his eyes just before they narrowed.

Still holding her close, he lifted his head.

Not everyone was occupied with celebratory champagne and pre-dinner hors d'oeuvres.

Frankie and Georgie had apparently been headed to the elevator to see the latest additions to Harry's art collection in the gallery above. Her mother and Harry, ten feet of tension separating them, had frozen in their tracks right behind them.

All were staring.

Tommi could pretty much imagine what was going through her sisters' minds at what they'd just witnessed. Her mom's thoughts were equally apparent as, her disquiet momentarily forgotten, she pressed her hand below her throat. Harry simply looked rather satisfied with what his interfering help had initiated between Tommi and the partner of the man he'd tried to set her up with.

Clearly calculating, Harry had just eyed an unsuspecting Frankie when Tommi felt Max's arms slip from around her.

With her family approaching, he took her right hand in his and leaned to whisper, "So we're official, then?"

There was no doubt in her mind what she wanted. "Absolutely."

"Good." He gave her hand a squeeze. "And by the way," he murmured, his lips warm against her ear, "thanks for the best Christmas I've ever had."

She would have thanked him back for the very same thing. She just didn't get the chance before her mom and older sisters converged to check out the beautiful ring he'd given her—and to welcome him into the family he'd once thought he'd never have.

* * * * *

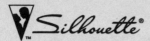
Silhouette®

COMING NEXT MONTH

Available December 28, 2010

SPECIAL EDITION

HARLEQUIN®

A Romance

FOR EVERY MOOD™

Spotlight on

Classic

Quintessential, modern love stories
that are romance at its finest.

See the next page
to enjoy a sneak peek from
the Harlequin Presents® series.

*Harlequin Presents® is thrilled
to introduce the first installment of
an epic tale of passion and drama by*
USA TODAY *Bestselling Author*
Penny Jordan!

*When buttoned-up Giselle first meets
the devastatingly handsome Saul Parenti,
the heat between them is explosive....*

"LET ME GET THIS STRAIGHT. Are you actually suggesting that I would stoop to that kind of game playing?"

Saul came out from behind his desk and walked toward her. Giselle could smell his hot male scent and it was making her dizzy, igniting a low, dull, pulsing ache that was taking over her whole body.

Giselle defended her suspicions. "You don't want me here."

"No," Saul agreed, "I don't."

And then he did what he had sworn he would not do, cursing himself beneath his breath as he reached for her, pulling her fiercely into his arms and kissing her with all the pent-up fury she had aroused in him from the moment he had first seen her.

Giselle certainly *wanted* to resist him. But the hand she raised to push him away developed a will of its own and was sliding along his bare arm beneath the sleeve of his shirt, and the body that should have been arching away from him was instead melting into him.

Beneath the pressure of his kiss he could feel and taste her gasp of undeniable response to him. He wanted to devour her, take her and drive them both until they were equally satiated—even whilst the anger within him that she should make him feel that way roared and burned its resentment of his need.

She was helpless, Giselle recognized, totally unable to withstand the storm lashing at her, able only to cling to the man who was the cause of it and pray that she would survive.

Somewhere else in the building a door banged. The sound exploded into the sensual tension that had enclosed them, driving them apart. Saul's chest was rising and falling as he fought for control; Giselle's whole body was trembling.

Without a word she turned and ran.

Find out what happens when Saul and Giselle succumb to their irresistible desire in

THE RELUCTANT SURRENDER

Available January 2011 from Harlequin Presents®

REQUEST YOUR FREE BOOKS!

2 FREE NOVELS PLUS 2 FREE GIFTS!

SPECIAL EDITION
Life, Love and Family!

SSE10R